COWBOY TARGET

BARB HAN

TORJAKE PUBLISHING

Editing: Ali Williams

Cover Design: Jacob's Cover Designs

To my family for unwavering love and support. I can't imagine doing life with anyone else. I love you guys with all my heart.

1

Brielle Anderson needed to quit her job. Period. This waking up before the sun had to go. She blinked blurry eyes and checked the clock on her nightstand only to get confirmation her eyes didn't need to be open. She should be sound asleep, lost somewhere deep in REM, but long workdays and travel left her unsure of what bed she was in, let alone which time zone. The changes were messing with her internal clock big time. It was a solid five a.m. in Cattle Cove and no one, repeat no one, should be awake at this hour on purpose.

Could she go back to sleep if she really put her mind to it? Brielle closed her eyes and gave it the old college try. She rolled over and lightly punched the pillow a few times before repositioning to get comfortable. Didn't work. She flipped onto her stomach. No good.

Her mind swirled back to the near miss she'd had on the highway on her way home from the office the other night. She'd nodded off for a second or two and woke up as one of those big SUVs cut her off. If she hadn't opened her eyes at that exact moment...

The whole experience had left her shaking. Panic seized her just thinking about what might have happened. Her reflexes weren't as fast as they should have been thanks to an overall lack of sleep. And yet, seeing those bright red brake lights at the end of her bumper had provided the jolt she needed. She'd swerved and slammed on her brakes in the nick of time.

Brielle was thankful to be alive. The whole experience had her questioning her life choices. She wasn't fresh out of college anymore. She'd been head down and guard up, prioritizing career over everything, including relationships. The one friend she had outside of work, her neighbor, could only be loosely classified as such. The recent and stunning realization she didn't love her job had sent her in a tailspin. Maybe it was her upcoming birthday and the fact she was turning a year older that was making life feel so...off track.

Then, there was a question that had been niggling at the back of her mind ever since. Would anyone even care if she was gone? Yes, her family would miss her. But her sister's pregnancy announcement, the fact she was starting a family of her own when Brielle hadn't gone on a date worthy of a second in years, weighed on her thoughts. It was odd because Brielle rarely ever thought about having a husband and kids or questioned her commitment to her job. She'd been soldiering on just like her dad had instilled in her. Her life had never felt empty before.

After tossing and turning a few more times, Brielle gave up the ghost and threw the covers off. She sat on the edge of the bed, wishing she could relax her body enough to go back to sleep. Late in the day, around four p.m., she would crash. Hard. There wasn't enough caffeine in the world to right her jet-lagged schedule or the way her mind kept turning over the situation.

So, of course, a food craving picked that moment to hit. It was probably stress eating, but she wanted a doughnut. And not just any doughnut, Dana's Do-nuts. She probably shouldn't give in. Being on the road, she had to constantly watch what she ate. Eating out three meals a day got old fast and it was a little too easy to grab whatever was convenient over making a healthy choice. She tried her best to save the treats for when she was home, so she wouldn't overdo it.

Between trying to go back to sleep and the possibility of eating one of Dana's finest, the doughnut won. She refused to feel guilty about indulging in one of her all-time favorites.

Off went her oversized sleepy shirt and shorts. On went her favorite jogging pants and sports bra. She threw on socks and was out the backdoor and onto the screened-in patio lacing up her tennis shoes before she could talk herself out of the trip.

The bike stored in her screened-in porch was ready and rearing to go. She hopped onto the two-wheeler and tucked the housekey into the pocket band of her joggers. It didn't take but a second to realize the tires were flat. Not surprising since she'd hardly been home and couldn't remember the last time she'd ridden the thing.

The pump was easy enough to find in the bench seat storage, though the fog in her brain wasn't so easy to shake. She managed, though. Within a couple of minutes, the tires were ready to go. The worse thing about owning a bike was having to constantly pump up the tires before a ride.

She replaced the pump and guided the bike out of the enclosure and around to the front of her house. Looking around, there were no lights on at this time of the morning in any of her neighbor's houses. This hour was reserved for bakers and ranchers. Having grown up in cattle ranching country, she was very familiar with the latter.

Halfway down the street, a cool breeze whipped through her hair. She pumped the pedals hard before relaxing and gliding down to the stop sign. She grabbed the rubber band from her wrist and pulled her hair up. Brielle would never consider herself a morning person. Although, she had to admit, they were nice. She enjoyed watching the occasional sunrise, and in Texas, there wasn't much that was more beautiful.

She pumped the pedals, forgetting just how much work riding a bike could be. The cardio would wake her up and have the added benefit of releasing her of guilt for eating a second doughnut. Something with sprinkles. She might as well go all-in at this point. She had to be burning a lot of calories with the way her thighs burned.

The fifteen-minute bike ride felt like an hour. By the time she reached Dana's Do-nuts, she was breathing so hard her ribs hurt. So, yeah, travel had interrupted her workout routine and she was getting out of shape fast. If this work schedule was going to keep up much longer, she needed to figure out how to find the discipline to exercise on the road. It wasn't like there weren't options. Every hotel had some type of workout facility. Granted, the quality of their gyms was all over the place; one would have a full-sized, fully equipped gym while another barely had two treadmills and a dozen free weights. But she could make anything happen if she put her mind to it. Life had proven she was just stubborn enough to meet any goal she set for herself.

It was about rallying enough self-discipline to get started. She parked her bike. Despite the recent crime spree in town, she didn't feel the need to lock up her transportation.

The hum of an engine caused her to turn. Headlights aimed right at her blinding her, as a truck pulled into a parking spot in front of Dana's. She brought her arm up to shield her eyes from the brightness. She turned her back to the vehicle and then headed toward the shop door as the driver seemed to catch on, cutting off his lights.

This early, she was probably going to be the first customer. The smell of freshly baked doughnuts and chocolate assaulted her senses, reminding her just how good this decision had been.

"Be right with you," Dana called out from the backroom.

"No rush," Brielle responded. There was something warm and familiar about being here. Maybe it was the fact she and her sister, Bethany, used to pop in before school sometimes. Brielle's sister was four years older, had met the love of her life in college, and moved to Tennessee where they'd both found jobs. Brielle rarely saw her sister anymore but that didn't stop them from staying in touch or being close.

The door opened behind her. The bell jingled. The heavy footsteps said the male driver was here for the same reason as her.

"Well, look who it is. Brielle Anderson." The familiar voice caused heat to crawl up her neck and her cheeks to burn. Now, she really felt like she was home.

"Dalton McGannon. That can't be you, can it?" She whirled around, trying to hide her body's reaction, masking it with the biggest smile she could muster. Bethany's high school boyfriend and Brielle's former secret crush had just entered the building.

"In the flesh," he said. Six-feet-four-inches of the hottest male flesh. She stopped herself right there and searched for a gold band on his left hand. He had to be married or committed by now. And, nope. No ring. Which didn't necessarily mean no significant other.

Oh, but Dalton had filled out in all the best possible ways. He might have been her sister's boyfriend, but that hadn't stopped Brielle from crushing on him. With those honey-brown eyes and just enough face scruff to be sexy, who could blame her?

He smiled and it caused a devastating reaction in the center of her chest.

"Wow. How long has it been?" she asked.

"Too long. I haven't seen you in forever." More of that smile and McGannon charm oozed off him.

"What are you doing here?" Needing to do something with her hands, she searched for her pants pockets before awkwardly remembering she had on joggers. *Smooth.*

"It's Miss Penny's birthday. I volunteered to pick up doughnuts." He had the kind of deep timbre that traveled all over Brielle's body, reminding her how long it had been since she'd had a boyfriend. Or even just a guy worthy of fancy date underwear.

"Wish her happy birthday for me, would you?" Miss Penny was one of her favorite people, but then again, most people loved the woman. She was warm, caring, and kind. Being around people like her was one of the many reasons people moved to a place like Cattle Cove to raise a family.

"Happy to." She laughed when he wiggled his eyebrows as he made a play on her words. All the McGannon boys were charming. Based on her interaction with Dalton, they'd carried the quality into adulthood. Did they go to some kind of special school for charisma? Jesus. Because her heart pounded the back of her ribcage when she stood anywhere near the man.

"Thank you. She's a special lady." She tried to ignore the fact he was wide awake at this early hour, whereas her brain wasn't quite firing on all cylinders yet.

"How long has it been since the last time we saw each other?" Dalton leaned a hip against the counter and rested his elbow on the partition. He had the gorgeous cowboy thing down pat with jeans, a cotton shirt and boots. And he filled out every inch of his clothes.

"Years." She couldn't count how many.

"How's your sister, by the way?"

"Bethany's fine. Happy. She and Tim are expecting in the spring."

"That's really cool news. Tell her congratulations for me." This conversation had turned them both into carrier pigeons, she mused. Being home was nice for a change. Sleeping in her own bed was something she could get used to. Or at least she hoped she could. The past few nights weren't great indications and she would be back on the road again in a few days.

"I will."

"How about you? I never see you in town. Do you live here?"

"My job keeps me on the road. I have a house on Staten Street about a fifteen-minute bike ride from here." She had no idea why she added the last detail except to say that, even now, Dalton had a tongue-tying effect on her. She over-explained when she was nervous. And forget about his smile. That show of perfectly straight, white teeth made his face even more devastatingly handsome.

"Brielle. Dalton." Dana appeared from the back room. Her gaze bounced from Dalton to Brielle and back. She quirked an eyebrow and Brielle could almost see the question forming in her mind, asking if the two of them were together.

"I'm alone. Just here for me," Brielle said quickly, her

cheeks flaming. Wasn't she scoring all the calm points today?

"What can I help you with?" Dana took a fresh pair of gloves off the counter and smiled, thankfully willing to let it go.

Brielle turned to face the counter, figuring shelves upon shelves of doughnuts would be enough to distract her from breathing in Dalton's warm and spicy scent.

She turned to face her. "I'll have two doughnuts with chocolate icing and sprinkles."

"That all?" Dana pulled the pair of doughnuts out and placed them in a small bag.

"That'll do it for me." She'd been planning on eating them right then and there but suddenly felt the need to leave. In fact, the faster she got out of there, the less she could embarrass herself. She'd done quite a number in front of Dalton as it was.

She paid and then turned, nearly bumping into Dalton. Breathing in his spicy scent conjured up all kinds of inappropriate images.

"Excuse me." She sidestepped at the same time as him.

"You'd make a great dance partner," he teased. They both knew he didn't dance. Or, at least, that's what her sister had claimed prom night.

"See you around." The casual line was meant to avoid an awkward goodbye.

"I'd like that," he said, causing another rush of warmth to climb up her neck.

Brielle had to talk herself off the ledge that was Dalton McGannon. Reminding herself that he'd been her sister's boyfriend in high school did little to quell the attraction she felt. What could she say? He had the whole tall, muscled, and gorgeous bit down. Embarrassing as it was, her body had a mind of its own when she was anywhere near him. Growing up had only changed the intensity. This seemed like a good time to remind herself he was being polite in saying he'd like to see her around. She probably imagined the look in his eyes that hinted there could be more to it.

She secured the doughnut bag in her basket and turned her bike around toward her street. Hopping on, she took a second to look into the doughnut shop window. A piece of her wished Dalton had checked her out and she shouldn't let herself feel disappointment that he hadn't.

DALTON STACKED five boxes of doughnuts on top of each other and headed out the door. Seeing Brielle was a blast from the past, and he told himself the aftershocks had been felt in his heart and not a surge of attraction. The last time he saw her, she'd been a teenager with braids and braces, all long legs and knobby knees.

Bethany, his girlfriend at that time and her sister, had been stuck babysitting Brielle more often than not. So Brielle had tagged along on half of their dates. Not an annoyance, so much as a constant presence who was always around, smiling. She'd been all bones and teeth back then.

Now, he noticed her. Not a good idea, he reminded himself as he walked to his truck where Bandit waited. The hundred- and forty-pound rescue sat tall in the passenger seat. He loved morning drives. Now, if Dalton could keep him off the doughnuts, they'd be in good shape.

He cracked a smile, thinking how nice it was to see Brielle again. Her back was to him and she'd stopped at the sign. Her feet were firmly planted to either side of her bike.

Didn't look like she was going to make it all the way home with the contents of her bag intact.

The hum of a vehicle's engine caught his attention as he secured the doughnuts in the back seat. Dalton did a double take when he saw blacked-out windows. From where he stood, the driver of the vehicle wouldn't be able to see him. And all he could see was the blackness of the SUV, which caused the tiny hairs on the back of his neck to prickle. There was nothing on the SUV to identify it. No bumper stickers. He had no idea who owned it, which didn't say much, considering he spent most of his time on the family's cattle ranch.

When the vehicle sped up and dovetailed toward Brielle, Dalton shouted. In the next instant, he was barreling toward her. The SUV blocked his view. His heart dropped when he heard a crunch and a scream.

Dalton bit out a few choice words, hoping Bandit wouldn't break the half-rolled up window trying to follow. His pulse skyrocketed as he gaited toward her and the vehicle reversed and then sped off. No plates.

Brielle was on the ground, five feet away from her bike, the back half of which was mangled.

"I'm okay," she said, rolling onto her back, wincing. She held up her right arm and showed him her elbow as he dropped to his knees beside her.

"Did he hit you anywhere?"

"No. I got off the bike in time and shoved my arm against the bumper. The momentum pushed me out of the way. What a crazy accident, and what a jerk for taking off like that." Her breath came out in gasps in between words. She was clearly shaken up.

"That was no accident."

She gasped. Eyes wide, she looked to be trying to process those words and coming up short.

"I saw the whole thing from the passenger side of my truck." He examined her arm and helped pick pebbles out of her skin. The cement burn ran wrist to elbow. She'd skinned her forearm.

"What do you mean that was no accident?" The shock on her face made him realize that she had no idea she'd been a target.

"There were no plates on the vehicle, and it swerved right at you at the last minute. That was intentional." He pulled out his cell. "And I'm calling Sheriff Justice."

"A vehicle just struck Brielle Anderson on her bicycle. I'm here with her on Main Street across from Dana's Do-nuts."

Brielle's heart still battered her ribs from the inside. The rest of her body was going to feel the pain from her fall later. And she wasn't sure she wanted to know why Dalton had the sheriff's contact information so readily available. Then her parents' warning came to mind. A couple of months ago, they told her to start locking her doors, which she had. Now that she really thought about it, she remembered them saying something about the McGannon family hitting a spell of bad luck, but that everyone should take note and be careful.

During college in Austin, Brielle developed the habit of locking doors. Honestly, she traveled so much that she was good about safety. She let her guard down this morning while distracted by seeing Dalton again, and it came back to bite her. But then, this was home despite not staying in contact with anyone other than her parents. She felt safe here. It was one of the main reasons she bought a house here. Eventually, she would fill it with a family and be glad she lived in a town known for family gatherings.

The fact her parents had to tell her about the McGannons pretty much made her the last person to know what was going on in Cattle Cove despite living here. All her friends had moved away to Austin or Dallas after graduating college. Her own sister had moved to Tennessee, fleeing the small town the minute she could. Only one of her neighbors was even remotely close in age and loosely considered a friend. Gabbie Gilbert moved to town six months ago after living in Dallas for the past five years. Her house was two doors down, and she almost constantly flew or drove back and forth to see her boyfriend—the boyfriend who refused to commit to the next step in their relationship, so she'd moved out and close to where she grew up in Austin.

Cattle Cove had an appeal Brielle couldn't pinpoint, except to say it was home. She stayed to be close to her parents. And, besides, work had her almost constantly on the go. She needed a place to plant her feet.

She tuned into Dalton's phone call as he gave the sheriff a description of the SUV. Brielle had been so blindsided by the whole episode she didn't get a good look at the vehicle or the driver. She was still trying to process Dalton's observation. Who would swerve *toward* her? Did a cat cross the road? A squirrel? There was no shortage of rabbits this time of year.

Surely, the driver took his or her eyes off the road for a few critical seconds. The person might have dropped something and then leaned over to get it. That happened...right?

Reminding herself to take it slow and breathe helped in most situations. Not so much this time. Because deep breaths meant taking in more of Dalton's spicy scent. Since this wasn't the time to dwell on an inconvenient attraction, she forced her thoughts away from her sister's ex.

There was not one person she could think of who would want to hurt her. And then she glanced at her bike. The back tire was so twisted up it might be beyond repair. And the frame? It looked like it got caught in a meat grinder.

Dalton ended the call and she could already hear the sirens in the distance.

"That was fast." She was thinking out loud and he seemed to realize it.

"Justice is on her way," he said, sizing Brielle up. "Are you hurt anywhere else besides your elbow?"

"Not that I know of. Maybe I should try to stand up." She tested her arms, but he was already shaking his head. Adrenaline would keep the pain at bay. That and shock. Later, she was going to feel it.

"Not a good idea." His gaze swept over her and through her, blazing a hot trail on her skin without intending to. That was just Dalton and his charm. He'd grown into his tall frame, filling it out nicely. The guy had been good looking before and now he was on a whole different level of gorgeous.

She nodded, shoving the attraction to the sideline while accepting the situation as much as her brain could handle under the circumstances. She was still processing the experience that could only be classified as surreal.

"Must have been kids joyriding or something," she reasoned.

"Or something is right. The jerk could've done a lot worse damage to you."

Her quick thinking saved her. As soon as she felt the vehicle come up on her from behind, getting too close for comfort, she strong-armed the bumper and used it to catapult herself off her bike. The landing had been hard and she didn't even want to think about the bruise that would show up later. But she was okay.

Dana bolted across the street from the doughnut shop. "What happened?"

The sound of sirens split the air and Brielle didn't want to shout over them. She twisted up her face and motioned in the general direction of the noise.

Dana nodded. She turned toward the noise and waved the first vehicle over with both arms in the air. The sheriff's SUV pulled onto the scene and parked behind Dalton's truck. Laney Justice stepped out of the vehicle. The sheriff wasn't more than five-feet-two-inches tall, but she walked with authority. Her confidence said she could handle herself in any situation. Most would describe her as tiny but mighty. She was attractive despite her serious expression. Her hair was pulled off her face in a low bun and she looked as compassionate as she was intense.

Lights whirled but at least she'd turned off the siren. There was a second one farther away. Ambulance?

"I'm okay," Brielle said first to Dalton.

"It's a precaution to have an EMT check you out." He put his hands up, palms out. "I requested it and I hope you'll agree to be checked over, if only for peace of mind."

He didn't say whose, his or hers, but she appreciated the fact he cared. And it probably would be a good idea to have someone take a look at her to make sure nothing was fractured. Considering no bones were sticking out, she figured she'd been spared a break. She'd slid on her forearm, skinning it worse than anything she'd suffered in grade school while playing tag on concrete.

Laney Justice introduced herself. She'd been quite a bit older than Brielle in school, but the Justice family had a good reputation in Cattle Cove and Brielle had a vague memory of her.

"Tell me in your own words what happened," Sheriff Justice said.

"I literally heard a vehicle get so close to me that I swerved to get out of its way. Headlights were blinding when I turned to try to get a look at the driver. I strong-armed the bumper, which sent me flying. My bike took the brunt of it. I'm shaken up but fine. That's about all. It all happened so fast."

"Can you tell me your name?" The sheriff stood, feet apart, and glanced around like she was surveying the surroundings.

"Brielle Anderson." She shot the sheriff a confused look.

"How did you land?" The sheriff took another tact. "On what body part?"

"Oh, I didn't hit my head if that's what you're asking. I can tell you a few things that might help. It's Friday morning. Early. I couldn't sleep. My internal clock is all mixed up from work travel, so I biked down to get a doughnut." That was probably more than the sheriff wanted to know, but it seemed to satisfy her concerns about possible head trauma.

Justice took a few notes on the notepad she'd pulled from her front pocket.

Dana stood, wringing her hands together. "Would you like anything? Water? Ice?"

"An ice pack would be nice if it's not too much trouble." Brielle's arm was starting to let her know it wasn't happy. She figured it was just the beginning, so she might as well head it off at the pass.

Dana waved her off. "I'll be right back." She turned tail toward the bakery.

"I apologize for the next few questions I have to ask," the sheriff continued.

Brielle tensed.

"Do you have a spouse, boyfriend, or significant other?"

"None of the above." Answering the routine-sounding question shouldn't bring more of that unwanted heat to her cheeks. And yet admitting to being all alone, did. The sensation was strange because she'd never been the kind of person who thought she needed someone else to complete her. And she still didn't. It must be the fact Dalton was here that caused the reaction. For reasons she couldn't explain, she wanted him to see her as extremely dateable.

"How about a recent breakup?"

"Nothing. I've been traveling too much for work to date and I have a rule against clients and coworkers." She didn't want to lift her eyes to meet Dalton's gaze for fear the flames would turn into an inferno. It was childish to want to impress him and harder still to admit to herself that she wanted to.

"Okay. Have you had any disagreements with coworkers? Neighbors? Friends?"

"My life is pretty boring actually. I haven't been in a fight with anyone." Admitting it made her want to go bungy jumping or skydiving. She was adventurous even if there was no evidence of that fact in her life lately. "I get along with my neighbors because I'm hardly ever home. They can't get too upset with me. I don't have any pets to make noise or dig up their yards. I have a yard service, so my grass never gets too high and they clean up the leaves when the trees shed." When she heard the words coming out of her mouth, she realized how empty her life sounded. Trying to rally an argument against it was no use. Being responsible was a good thing. Being in her twenties without an ounce of adventure wasn't.

She *had* become boring and she'd just said it out loud. It had become so easy to pop a pre-made meal from one of those farm-to-table services into the microwave and binge watch a series until she fell asleep. Occasionally, she had a glass of wine on the back porch. *Wow. Way to spice it up.*

Basically, she was a responsible adult. So, why did that sound more boring than watching paint dry?

And why did it embarrass her so much to admit all this in front of Dalton?

DALTON'S MIND RACED. It was probably because his family had seen more than their fair share of crime in recent weeks, but he didn't trust the driver of the SUV. The person had to be up to something. The question was...was this a random opportunity?

Dana returned with a bag of ice and a handful of waters as the ambulance roared onto the scene.

"These are for whoever wants them," she said, holding out the bottles.

He took them out of her hands, and she gave over the ice.

Brielle touched the cold bag to her forearm, and then sucked in a burst of air. This was probably just the beginning of the pain she was going to feel later after taking the tumble off her bike. If she hadn't strong-armed the SUV...

Dalton didn't even want to think about what could have happened. Years might have passed but he still felt a certain protective instinct over Brielle.

Joel Hayden hopped out of the driver's seat of the ambulance and rushed over, emergency medical bag in hand. He was stocky and had been a decent football player. His Friday night lights career ended with injuries to both knees. "What happened?"

Dalton filled him in while Sheriff Justice asked a few more routine-sounding questions. When Justice closed her notepad before tucking it into her pocket, Joel went to work on Brielle. Dana had retreated to the front of her shop, watching from a distance as Dalton gave his statement.

"Have there been any other reports of wild driving tonight?" he asked the sheriff.

"No. None." She had the all-too-familiar frustration in her voice. Not again. Life had been quiet in Cattle Cove lately, and it was a much-needed break after the recent spate of crimes—crimes that had impacted his family firsthand.

Justice exhaled.

"What are the chances a kid stole his dad's SUV and went for a joyride?" he asked.

"That's always a possibility." She didn't sound convinced.

"Brielle is as sweet as they come. I can't imagine anyone being upset with her, let alone pulling something like this." Despite not being around her in the past ten years, his impression of her was that she hadn't changed. She'd grown up. That was for sure. And her smile was even brighter if that was possible. She'd filled out too. And there were other attributes he didn't want to allow himself to notice.

"I think we both know decent people can end up a target as easily as everyone else." Justice's point was spot on. "What can you tell me about the victim?"

"Not much more than I already did. She's always been a good kid." Somehow the word didn't fit her anymore.

"How do the two of you know each other?"

"I dated her sister a million years ago. High school," he clarified. "She tagged along most of the time."

"And did the two of you stay in touch?"

"This is the first time I've talked to her in more years than I can count." He was embarrassed to realize he didn't even know she had a house in town. Of course, he kept to the ranch. The family business—empire as some would call it—took up most of his time and there wasn't much reason for him to leave the property. Each of his brothers and cousins had a home built in a different spot on the property. The family had the shock of finding out they had a half-brother. Him and his daughter had been welcomed into the family and were in the process of finding a place to build. "You know how it is after school. People go their separate ways."

Justice nodded.

Dalton glanced back to find Joel closing up his medical bag. They weren't standing close enough for Dalton to catch what was being said, but it looked like good news. Joel held out his arm and Brielle took it, using it to help hoist her to standing.

The smile Joel gave shouldn't irritate Dalton as much as it did.

3

"Thank you." Brielle had forgotten that Joel had stayed in town after graduation. He'd been a year ahead of her in school.

"Maybe I'll see you around sometime." Joel smiled and glanced at his uniform. "When I'm not wearing one of these."

"That'd be nice. I hardly ever talk to anyone I knew from school anymore."

Joel's offer didn't sit well with at least one other person. Brielle picked up on tension radiating from Dalton and she had no idea what caused the change in temperature. Then again, he could be an intense person when he wanted to. It was another one of those McGannon family traits.

"See you around," Joel said before shaking Dalton's hand, nodding toward the sheriff, and returning to his ambulance.

Dalton grumbled something under his breath that she couldn't make out. She told herself to ask him about it later.

"Is this the first time anything like this has happened?" the sheriff asked, redirecting the conversation back on track.

"Yes...actually, no. The other night I could've sworn someone was in my house. I called your office." It wasn't exactly the same thing.

"I heard you had rats in your attic." The sheriff's face twisted and one of her eyebrows arched.

"Deputy Curtis tried to convince me the same thing. I could've sworn it was more than that, but he didn't find any signs of a break-in, so I let it go and forgot all about it after making a note to call the exterminator," Brielle admitted. "It was creepy, though."

"Mind if I swing by and take a look for myself?" The sheriff didn't seem the type to take something like this lightly on her watch.

"Not at all." In fact, she wanted to add that she'd feel a lot safer if Justice did. "I was headed home..."

Brielle looked over at her broken bike.

"I can give you a ride," Justice offered.

"Can I have a second with the victim?" Dalton had been quiet for the last few minutes. Brooding?

Sheriff Justice nodded. "I want to take a couple of pictures of the scene. Then, I'll start the report in my vehicle."

"If you leave the back open, I'll bring her bike over and load it up," Dalton offered. No worries about destroying any fingerprints.

"Thank you," Justice said before heading over to the scene and pulling out her phone, no doubt for the camera feature.

"You thought someone was in your house the other night? And now this?" Dalton's words weren't accusatory so much as just going through the facts.

"I thought I was overreacting after the deputy gave his assessment. But, yeah."

"Did he even check your attic?" Now, there was frustration in Dalton's voice. A woman calls in a noise concern and suddenly she's paranoid. He made a point. If she'd been a man would the deputy have been so quick to dismiss her complaint? The deputy had taken her statement and checked her house while she waited in the kitchen.

"Have you seen any rat droppings?" Dalton asked.

"Not downstairs. I didn't go in the attic. It creeps me out." As far as embarrassing admissions went, she was basically spilling all of hers in one fell swoop.

"I have doughnuts to deliver and a dog in my pick up." Dalton rubbed the scruff on his chin. "And then you just picked yourself up a houseguest."

"I'll be fine. You don't have to go to any trouble, Dal—"

"It's no trouble and I'm not doing it for you." He winked and more of that McGannon charm rolled off him.

Her heart did a little dance and she knew better than to read more into it. Dalton cared about her like a little sister and he was being protective. Thinking it was more than that would only lead to disappointment.

"Then, who?" She decided to play along, needing a little humor after the morning's shakeup.

"Me. Of course."

"Care to explain?"

"Okay. Here's the deal. If I leave you and don't make absolutely certain that you're okay, I won't be able to sleep."

"It's morning. You will have forgotten all about this by nightfall." She knew he wouldn't, but she was teasing him about it anyway.

"Not a chance." His smile disappeared and his gaze narrowed, causing her heart to give another little flip. "Seriously, though. This could have ended badly and you might not be out of danger. Until I know for certain, I'd like to hang around."

Conversation stopped as the sheriff walked past them.

"I'd like to check out your attic myself once the sheriff is done. See for myself if the rat theory holds true."

"Okay." She wasn't about to turn down help. Her father would volunteer to do it but he was getting older and she didn't like him climbing up the rickety ladder that had to be pulled down from the ceiling. Her attic was unfinished and it would be so easy to lose balance and put a foot through the sheetrock. Or fall through entirely for that matter.

Dalton fished his phone out of his pocket and handed it over after unlocking the screen. "Mind putting in your contact information? It'll be faster if you do it. Believe me," he said. "All I'm good for with one of those is making a call and the occasional text."

"Cell service always was spotty on the ranch." Plus, he wasn't exactly the type to be on a device or piece of technology all day. Their fingers grazed and she felt the roughness to his touch, a sign he worked with his hands. Electricity pulsed from the point of contact running up her arm and exploding in the center of her chest. She'd never felt so much chemistry in one touch before and it startled her.

Brielle entered her address and cell number before returning the phone to its owner. "There you go." She was careful not to graze fingers again and risk more of that electricity shooting through her. Besides, adrenaline was wearing thin and she was starting to feel those aches and pains from the fall.

"I shouldn't be long." He made the promise and then turned toward his truck.

"Are you taking off now?"

"I'd like to try to make it to your house before the sheriff leaves. Plus, my dog is in the truck and I don't want to leave him alone any longer."

The thought comforted her.

In the next moment, Dalton was inside his pickup and headed in the opposite direction.

DALTON MADE it to the ranch in record time. Even so, he was late. Rather than take a razzing for it, he came clean about witnessing an accident. "Everyone is okay. It was a hit and run."

The kitchen was full and the chatter loud. Miss Penny beamed as she made her rounds, offering everyone a cup of coffee.

"It's your turn to be spoiled," Dalton said as he set the boxes of doughnuts onto the table. "Why don't you take a seat?"

The doughnuts had been ordered ahead and the top box had her favorite, a cinnamon cake doughnut, with a couple of candles on it. Dalton retrieved a box of matches from the junk drawer in the center island.

All six of Dalton's brothers were there, including the newest one, as well as their five cousins. Their father sat at the head of the table next to an empty seat reserved for Miss Penny. Clive McGannon had made the ranch he'd been handed a success. His brother, Donny, had cashed out his inheritance, walked out on his five sons, and then wasted all his money gambling. He'd shown up with his hand out a few years ago and had been angling for more control over the ranch ever since.

Uncle Donny was currently in jail for attempted murder.

No bail had been set. And even though his sons had been raised by Dalton's father, they still felt a sense of loyalty to their own. The pending case was the reason for the tension in the room among brothers and cousins. And it was so thick right now he could cut it with a knife. So, he got the festivities going.

The ranch foreman, Hawk, was there. He'd been nick-named for the fact nothing got past him. He stood in the background until Dalton's father urged him to take a seat at the family table. He chose one at the opposite end and a look passed between the two men Dalton made a note to ask about later.

Miss Penny shocked everyone by foregoing the chair by her longtime employer and friend in order to sit next to Hawk. But then, the two had been friends for thirty-odd years. And speculation said they'd become closer than that in recent months.

"The sheriff is coming over tomorrow morning." His dad clasped his hands and placed them on top of the large hand-carved wooden table that easily seated a dozen on each side, leaving the pair of ends for their dad and Miss Penny.

The fact his dad didn't say anything else told Dalton all he needed to know about why the sheriff was coming.

Two of Daltons' cousins, Reed and Brant, exchanged a look. The other three, Hayden, Coby, and Cage, stared intensely at the table. No one, including Dalton and his brothers, wanted Donny McGannon to be guilty of attempted murder. Not because he was a trusted family member, but because he was father to five of the men sitting at the table. Men who Dalton and his brothers had grown up with side-by-side, working the ranch. Not only close family but friends too. And the man their father was accused of trying to murder was the person who'd raised them. So, the word *complicated* didn't begin to describe the situation or the feelings in the room.

"I just thought everyone should know where the case stood," Dad said. He let another moment pass before he spoke. Then, he clapped his hands together one time and smiled. His eyes lit up and his entire demeanor changed when he added, "We have a very special person to celebrate this morning."

"Here, here," a few of the guys said in unison, raising up a coffee cup in salute.

Miss Penny blushed. She had the kind of clear green eyes that could see right through a person and she'd seen through Dalton, his brothers, and his cousins' BS throughout their childhood and teenage years. Out of respect, no one pushed her buttons, but she also ran a tight ship. One that had every male who came inside the house lining up their boots perfectly on the back porch. She was a simple person but that didn't mean she wasn't quick minded and intelligent. More than not, she had on a blouse with jeans, often wearing her favorite apron that spelled out the word, *BOSS*. It was true. She was the head honcho of all things inside the big house. Outside was Dad's terrain.

Levi, the oldest brother until Kurt came out of the blue recently, had lit the candles on Miss Penny's favorite doughnut. In a sound worse than a chainsaw being used on concrete, everyone erupted into the familiar birthday tune.

Miss Penny was a sport. She beamed. Never one for the spotlight for long, she immediately blew out the candles. "Don't let the doughnuts dry up, boys."

Hawk picked her mug up off the table and refilled it, before bringing it back and setting it on the table next to her. Her cheeks could have lit a match for how brightly they burned. And if all that sweetness didn't make him want gag, several of his brothers leaned in and planted a kiss on their new wives.

And since that seemed like as good a time as any, Dalton slipped out the back door and grabbed Bandit. He could text Levi or A.J. once he arrived in town to let them know he wasn't coming back to work today. There was a stop he wanted to make on the way to Brielle's. He wanted to put a smile on her face again after what had to be a truly scary morning for her.

The stop was on the way and it took less than five minutes. By the time he arrived in front of her house, the sheriff was sitting in her SUV, typing away into the laptop affixed to her dashboard.

She glanced up as he and Bandit neared. He waved and she did the same. He wanted to know what time she planned on being at the ranch tomorrow morning to revisit the scene of the accident. He used the term loosely, and it was more hope than fact.

And all that did was remind him to reach out to one of his brothers before he forgot. He fished his cell out of his front pocket, and then fired off a text, holding onto the bag in the process. No one was on the clock at the ranch. The text was courtesy. McGannons looked out for each other.

Brielle lived in one of those old Victorian houses with a large front porch and latticework wrapping around the edges. There'd been some debate over trying to file paperwork to designate this neighborhood as historically significant. From a homeowner's point of view, the proclamation could make it a pain in the neck to get any work done since period details would have to be honored. From a financial perspective, though, the value of the neighborhood would go up as a piece of the town's history would be preserved.

The shingles on this house had a recent coat of gray

paint along with the white shudders. The porch had painted concrete that coordinated with the shingles. A white porch swing that hung by chains had colorful throw pillows on it. Dalton had no idea what the big interest in throw pillows was, but he couldn't deny they brightened up the area. The rest of the decoration matched the style of the house, including fresh flowers in a vase. This was a place of arches, irregular shapes, and textured shingles. The porch was wraparound and the kind he could envision people sitting on for hours in rocking chairs as folks walked by.

The place was beautiful by most standards, and yet all he could think about was the joy that would come with hundred-plus-year-old plumbing.

Bandit at his side, he knocked on the front door, thinking how long it had been since he'd seen Brielle and how random it was that they were both at the same doughnut shop. To be fair, Dana's Do-nuts was the best and he stopped by there at least once a month and hadn't seen hide nor hair of Brielle. She seemed to love the place too. At least, she and her sister had years ago.

"Coming." Brielle's now very grown-up voice traveled through the door and the effect it had on his body put him on edge.

She opened the door and her gaze homed in on the bag in his hand, and then the dog by his side.

"You brought doughnuts?" Dalton never thought he'd used the word *glee* to describe a grown woman, except it was the best one to describe her reaction to the bag from Dana's, and it made him feel so very pleased that he'd stopped off to pick them up.

"Figured you biked all the way into town and yours ended up on the pavement. Consider these your replacement set."

The way her smile danced in her eyes warmed his heart.

"I'm guessing this is your dog." She reached down and patted Bandit.

"Best rescue in Texas. Don't tell my brothers. They all think their dogs are the best. Don't even come close to my Bandit."

She smiled.

"In that case, come on in." She took a step back and opened the door wide. "Just make sure and lock it for me if you don't mind."

Locking doors was new in Cattle Cove. He twisted the knob and heard the snick of the lock. Dalton's cell buzzed as he handed over the bag, which Brielle took with enthusiasm.

"These will go best with coffee. Follow me." She hop-walked and he realized she was struggling a little bit.

Instead of answering the call, he moved beside her and held out his arm for her to lean on. The electricity that shot through his arm further fueled his frustration. This was little Brielle Anderson, his mind reasoned. The younger sister of a person he dated in high school. Yes, she was beautiful with those hazel eyes surrounded by thick, black lashes. Her silky russet locks and creamy skin weren't things he wanted to notice. Neither was the dotting of freckles across the bridge of her nose. And he sure didn't want to pay attention to those cherry lips of hers.

And yet, that's exactly what he did.

4

T he phrase, *walk it off,* never had more meaning to Dalton than it did right then. Despite his frustration, the corners of his mouth betrayed him, upturning in a grin the minute Brielle looked up at him. His chest clenched too and that meant he was in serious trouble when it came to the hazel-eyed beauty.

"If you want to take a seat and point me in a direction, I'll get the coffee." He helped her ease into a chair at the four-top table pushed up against an ornate kitchen window. And to make matters worse, his voice sounded husky. *Well played, Dalton. Way to keep your emotions in check with your ex-girlfriend's little sister.*

To make matters even worse for him, those eyes were glittery and there was nothing 'little sister' about Brielle. "Over there."

She pointed. He followed the trail. These old houses weren't known for having the biggest kitchens and this one wouldn't fit half of his brothers. It was cozy, though. And had plenty of room for the two of them and Bandit, who curled in a ball underneath the table.

"How's your sister?" He didn't care and he realized he'd asked the same question at the donut shop. It seemed like the polite thing to ask.

"Good." Brielle took a bite of doughnut and coughed.

He glanced over in time to catch her cheeks blazing. Hells bells, he didn't want her to be embarrassed around him. They had history and had known each other for what felt like forever. He made two cups of coffee with those pod thingies. "Cream? Sugar?"

"I like mine black."

"Same." That was easy. He brought the mugs over and set hers down on the table next to her.

She picked it up with both hands and practically mewled with pleasure after taking the first sip. Not a sound he needed replaying in his head when he thought about her later.

"She loves where she lives in Nashville," Brielle continued. "And her husband is the perfect fit for her. They're two peas in a pod."

She glanced over at him as he took a seat. "Sorry if this isn't what you wanted to hear."

He brushed the comment off with the wave of his hand. "We dated in high school. That was a long time ago. Tell me more."

"She's over the moon about the baby and a little bit scared at the prospect of taking care of a tiny little human." She took another bite of doughnut and then washed it down with more coffee. The bandage on her arm, wrist to elbow, a reminder of the seriousness of what had gone down.

"I can only imagine." He must've made a face because she responded with a surprised look on her face.

"What? You don't want a family?"

"Never think about it."

"Seriously?"

"Do you?"

Her lips compressed in the way they did when she didn't want to admit something.

"Maybe. Someday. Definitely not right now." She flashed her eyes at him. "I'm not even dating anyone seriously. Or dating much at all, if I'm honest."

"You?" He could hardly believe there weren't troves of guys lining up to spend time with her. There was so much more to her than beauty. Although, she had that in spades. She was kind, if a little bit shy. And smart. Her sister had always talked about how intelligent Brielle was and he'd seen glimpses of it years ago.

"Don't say it like that. My career keeps me busy twenty-four-seven and I don't need another person in my life to make me a whole person." She said that last part a little too defensively. Then she turned the tables. "What about you? I'm guessing half the female population of Cattle Cove is trying to get your attention."

"Which isn't all that impressive when you consider the average age is fifty-two," he teased.

She laughed and the sound had a musical quality.

"Be serious," she insisted.

"I am. Have you checked out the local dating scene? It's a little tough to swipe right in a town where most of the females are already married and old enough to be your mother."

"Okay. Point taken. The average age in town is..."

"Geriatric."

"Fifty-two isn't *that* old," she defended with a fiery spark in her eyes—a spark that lit a campfire in his chest. The lighthearted teasing brought down the tension from earlier a few notches but was doing nothing to quell the attraction brewing between them.

"There's nothing wrong with being fifty-two or dating someone who is, but I'm not quite out of my twenties yet."

"Fair enough." She smiled and a bomb detonated in his chest.

"In all seriousness, it's not easy to meet someone in Cattle Cove that's close to my age or doesn't already know my family. Most of the people I knew growing up moved away to go to school or join the service and haven't come back. I imagine they will once they're ready to settle down, which is too late for a first date with me. Austin isn't a bad drive, and neither is Houston. I take a weekend here and there to meet people, which has the added bonus of it taking a minute for some to realize who I am."

"Oh. Right. McGannon. Must be tough to have such a recognizable last name. We all grew up together and not one of you guys ever acted hoity-toity, so it was easy to forget how successful your family is."

He appreciated the explanation and the sentiment. Most people just called them rich. Others decided they were all spoiled because they mostly kept to themselves. Owning and operating a multimillion-dollar cattle ranch took more time and energy than most realized. And it seemed like everyone in Cattle Cove knew their business anyway. Dalton and his brothers generally kept a low profile.

"I remember how early you guys used to get up. My sister said you all worked the ranch before school," she said on a sigh.

"When we didn't have sports in the morning. Between my brothers and cousins, we figured it out and made sure there was coverage so we could take part in sports." He took a sip of coffee, enjoying the burn on his throat. It was nice to have a casual conversation.

"As memory serves, you were all really good at them too."

"Ryan had the most talent." His brother had turned down a shot at the majors to become a rancher and had no regrets.

"Oh, I remember. Everyone thought he was crazy." She shrugged. "I think it would be crazier not to follow your dreams or live your true self. You know?"

"That, I do." His brother loved baseball, but he loved the land more, and he wanted to keep the sport pure by not mixing his livelihood with it.

"I don't think I ever thanked you for letting me tag along with you and my sister on all your dates." More of that red blush crawled up her neck.

And it stirred his heart.

~

IT HAD BEEN A ROUGH MORNING. Brielle wanted so much to believe her physical reaction to Dalton was nothing more than simple proof of life. She'd had a near miss and now biology had kicked in, causing her to be attracted to the first good-looking and physically capable guy she saw. Seriously attracted.

Dalton had the whole thick lips with a face of hard angles and sharp planes in spades. Most would consider him gorgeous. He'd laugh if he heard himself described that way. Didn't make it less true, though. The man could be on a billboard.

But that wasn't the reason for her crush. He had a magnetism and charm beyond anything she'd ever experienced in a person. He was more than just a hot bod with a pretty face. She'd seen him rescue countless animals from the side of the road. Case in point, Bandit here.

The dog couldn't have found a more loving home. The McGannons, Dalton included, took care of all the creatures who needed them. The family had always been especially fond of dogs and horses, but they'd take care of anything that needed help. She once saw them nurse a raccoon back to health before releasing it only to have it come back for treats once a day.

So, yeah, they were good people. Dalton was a good person. And it was nice to see that hadn't changed about him. Her sister had changed since tying the knot three years ago. Nashville was all she could talk about, detailing out every reason why it was great there and so much better than home. Brielle couldn't count the number of times her sister said she never wanted to come back to Cattle Cove. Not even to visit their aging parents because the town was so boring.

"You never wanted to leave?" Curiosity was getting the best of Brielle and she wanted to get to know more of the grown-up version of Dalton.

"This is my home. I love the land. My family is here. And, besides, where else would I go? There isn't a place I can think of that has such a wide-open sky. I step outside and I can breathe. And don't even get me started on the stars at night."

Brielle was rocking her head in agreement. "It's nice not to have to defend my reasons for sticking around to someone for a change."

"Your sister didn't like it here?"

"Are you kidding me? She couldn't leave fast enough. Said this place was too quiet and it suffocated her."

"Strange. She never said anything to me about it when

we dated. In fact, she gave me the impression she loved it here."

"You were pretty clear on where you stood. I doubt she'd give away her true thoughts if it meant the possibility of losing you."

"I wouldn't break up with her over whether or not she liked being here." He rubbed the scruff on his chin. "But the relationship wouldn't have gone anywhere. Not that it would have anyway. We were kids back then. Both of us had a lot of growing up to do before we'd be ready to commit to someone long-term." He laughed. "Hell, I'm staring down thirty and the thought of marriage is enough to make me loosen my collar."

Brielle took a sip of coffee, figuring Dalton wasn't the marrying type. Was she?

"What about you?" He turned the tables.

She almost spit out her coffee at the question. Rather than get into that with him, she picked up one of her doughnuts and took a bite. "This is amazing. Thank you for bringing these."

His smirk said he realized she'd just dodged his question.

"If you'll point me to the attic, I'd like to check it out for myself," he said.

She started to get up but he stopped her by putting his palm out.

"Finish your breakfast. You deserve it after the morning you've had."

Was it wrong that she didn't need a whole lot of convincing?

"A bright spot was running into you again and I haven't seen Joel in ages. I didn't realize he still lived here."

A look passed behind Dalton's eyes at the mention of

Joel. It was probably just wishful thinking on her part, but he looked a little jealous there for a split second before recovering.

"Good to see you again too," he mumbled.

"Second story in the hallway leading toward the master bedroom. You can't miss it," she said.

"All right. I'll head up and report back." He looked to Bandit. "Keep her company, will you, buddy?"

Bandit wagged his tail at the attention.

Dalton set his coffee cup down and disappeared down the hallway. The old wood flooring groaned under his heft and Brielle thought about how much she needed to feel that weight on top of her, pressing her into the mattress.

More of that proof of life? Or had the once-crush turned into a full-on attraction? *Waste of time*, she thought. He was clear about not wanting a serious relationship. Not that she did. But there was no point in going into one that wouldn't go anywhere.

Or maybe that's just what she needed. A fling. Someone to break the non-dating streak and give her a reason to pull her nice boots out of the closet for a change.

And that's exactly where she'd leave the thought. Right there on the kitchen floor after dropping it.

She reached for her laptop as she polished off the first doughnut. Chocolate. Sprinkles. She was impressed he'd gotten her order right. But then, he was probably just attentive, and she had been standing right in front of him in line at Dana's. Considering they'd been the only two in the shop, she decided not to be too flattered.

Brielle took another sip of coffee and polished off the second doughnut, thankful no one was there to judge. Besides, with the morning she'd had, she earned the epic sugar rush. Shifting in her seat, her hip reminded her just how hard the fall had been. Despite wearing joggers, she'd managed to skin her outer thigh. So, that was great. Sleeping on her side tonight was going to be fun. If by fun she meant running her body through a cheese grater.

The house creaked and groaned as she heard Dalton move around. She appreciated his willingness to double-check the deputy's work. He'd been in a hurry when she called. She'd blamed her parents for making her paranoid, but now she wondered if there hadn't been more to it.

She opened her inbox and saw the number 147. How could any person collect that many e-mails in the span of... she checked the time...fifteen hours? Didn't people sleep anymore? She almost laughed out loud. She, of all people, shouldn't be complaining about other people's lack of sleep considering she seemed to have lost her ability to get a straight eight hours.

Her cell buzzed. She retrieved it and checked the screen. There was a message from Gabbie.

Any chance I can borrow your car later? Mine crapped out and I need to get to the airport. I'll be gone for two days, work and fun. That a problem?

Brielle typed a response.

Take it. Keys are under the planter, like usual.

She could always borrow her mom's car if she needed to but the work from home edict would give her a couple of days where she didn't need to be anywhere. The security system was being updated at work and no one was required to come into the building. After sending the message, she thought about her bike. Her only other form of transportation was clearly not an option. But she could get delivery for dinner.

The stairs creaked and she could hear Dalton's footsteps coming down the hall a few seconds later. He moved around in the other rooms before appearing in the doorway. He put his arms up over his head, crossing his hands at his wrists and grabbing onto the molding.

"Do you want the good news or the bad news?" he asked.

"Good."

"There are no rats."

"What's the bad news?"

"I just told you."

No rats meant something else had been in her attic and the deputy had either lied or been too lazy to check.

"I already texted the sheriff," he added.

5

"Have you thought about installing an alarm system?" Dalton thought about pulling a few strings and speeding up the job.

"Not really. Honestly, that's half the reason I live in Cattle Cove. It's been safe." She held up her hand, palm up. "I know that's changed recently but it's still shocking. You know?"

He nodded.

Glancing out the window, he saw a woman walking a little too closely to Brielle's house for comfort. She moved around the back of the home and opened the door to the porch enough to bend down and retrieve an object. He couldn't see what she palmed as he moved to the window to get a better look.

"What is it?" Brielle asked, concern wrinkling her forehead.

"Someone is...hold on—"

"It's my neighbor. It's fine. She asked to borrow my car. I keep a key out there for her for when she needs it."

Dalton's blood pressure shot up and his protective

instincts flared. He exhaled before flexing and releasing his fingers a few times to work out some of the tension. "About that alarm." He circled the conversation back. "What do you think about getting one now?"

She frowned. "It's probably a good idea. Honestly, I haven't given it much thought until recently."

The town of Cattle Cove would have to rebrand itself if the crime spree continued. It would no longer be able to consider itself a safe place to raise a family.

"I'm probably being naïve here," she continued, "but there has to be a possibility the run-in this morning had to do with teenagers pulling a prank or getting too wild."

"Then why remove the plates?" he asked.

"They probably didn't want to get caught."

"What about the possibility of someone inside your home?"

"Could've been the wind...right? You said yourself there were no signs of rats in the attic. I didn't actually see anyone come in or out of the house. Or anyone inside the house for that matter." He understood her need to think through all the possibilities and her brain's natural response to want to block out the ones that mean someone was aggressively after her.

"You're the one who heard the noises. I can't speak for those. As far as kids joyriding, it's possible, if unlikely."

She picked up the coffee mug and rolled it around in her palms. After taking a deep breath, she said, "Someone could've stolen the vehicle and been joyriding from the night before. Or still drunk."

"Again, the plates."

Another sharp breath. "That explains how it couldn't be a drunk driver but not necessarily someone who intended to go out and vandalize or cause havoc. We don't know what the driver's true intentions were. He or she could have been trying to scare me. It makes the person a jerk-off but not someone attempting murder."

Dalton nodded. He didn't want to rain on her parade by continuing to point to the fact this looked like the job of someone who, at the very least, had an acquaintance with her. Especially considering the possible break-in to her home. Her brain wasn't processing the situation and the shock most likely hadn't worn off. Since they were getting nowhere and she yawned for the third time in ten minutes, he figured a change of subject would be more productive at this point. Or rest.

When she covered her fourth yawn, he decided to go for the second thought. "What do you think about lying down and trying to take a nap?"

"What will you do?" Big eyes blinked up at him.

"I can stick around, if that's what you're worried about," he offered.

"Will you come lie down with me?" She quickly clarified. "On top of the covers. Or whatever." More of that red blush crawled up her neck to her checks and his heart took another hit.

"Yes." His voice cracked on the word, so he cleared his throat to ease the sudden dryness. This seemed like a good time to remind himself she was Bethany's kid sister.

He walked over to her and held out an arm.

"The coffee did nothing to wake me up. I think my adrenaline has faded and I'm starting to feel every bump, scrape and bruise." She took his offering and more of that electricity zipped through him.

"Sounds about right. Let's get you to bed." He flashed a smile the second he heard how that sounded. "To *your* bed."

Then, he laughed. "Well, that didn't sound any better, did it?"

"I knew what you meant." She winced as she put weight on her right side.

"This might be less painful and faster all around." He picked her up, careful to make sure her left side was against his chest.

She didn't speak as he carried her up the stairs but he could feel her pulse racing. It was most likely from the pain and not because of their close proximity.

He eased her onto the bed and she rolled onto her good side.

"Better?" he asked.

"Much."

"Good." Dalton glanced down at his dog, who was ready to hop onto the bed. "Any rules about where Bandit sleeps?"

"He's welcome anywhere he wants to go."

Dalton gave Bandit the okay to hop onto the bed and he quickly made himself comfortable after turning around several times. He curled up against the backs of Brielle's knees.

"Want me to close the blinds?" he asked.

"If you don't mind," she said. "I doubt I'll be able to sleep, but it'll be nice to rest for a little while."

"Nah." It was no trouble. He went around closing the blinds, plunging the room into darkness. He cracked the bedroom door before toeing off his boots and joining Brielle on the other side of the bed. He was a big guy, which made the king-sized be feel like a queen. Between Dalton, her and Bandit, there wasn't enough free space to fill a postage stamp. She didn't seem to mind.

Despite her protest only a minute ago, her steady, even breathing said she was out. Dalton wished he'd brought up the laptop he'd seen on the kitchen table. He could flip through messages on his phone while he gave her space to sleep. He'd leave but wanted to be around when she woke up. After what she went through, he figured her brain would start processing the threat.

In his heart of hearts, he didn't believe this was random. Opportunistic? Possibly. Which meant she knew the person who'd attempted to hurt her, if not kill her. In his heart of hearts, he believed the driver turned the steering wheel toward her on purpose.

Of course, the SUV might have swerved at the last minute anyway. The driver could have been trying to scare her. Threaten her?

Without any arguments or ex-boyfriends to go on, the obvious choices were knocked out. He needed to find out what she did for a living. Maybe her line of work put her in harm's way without realizing it.

With enough digging, he might uncover a suspect or two. People could be crazy. He had the recent experiences of his family as proof. Several members had been targeted or tangled up in crimes.

When Brielle woke from her nap, he needed to talk to her a little bit more about her friends and get a little more information about her ex-boyfriends. It was for the case, he tried to convince himself, and not because he wanted to know the type of people she let in her life.

He chalked it up to his protective instincts that he still had for his ex's kid sister. Although, it wasn't just a protective instinct that made him react to Brielle's curves or the way her flowery scent filled his senses and stirred his heart.

BRIELLE BLINKED HER EYES OPEN. Lying next to her was her childhood crush. Dalton McGannon. What a strange twist of fate. The two lived in the same town for years and literally never crossed paths. Until now.

As her gaze focused, she caught sight of him staring at his screen. Deep worry lines scored his forehead and he frowned.

"What's going on?" She eased up to sitting position careful not to anger the massive bruise she clearly had on her right hip. She could definitely feel that one.

Dalton returned a text, and then lowered the phone. "The sheriff has been trying to reach you. She couldn't get hold of you, so she tried my cell. Your vehicle was found."

Maybe it was because he stopped right there that caused her to finish the sentence for him in her mind. She struggled to find the words. Then came, "Gabbie?"

He shook his head. "I'm sorry."

A mix of anger and sadness rushed through her, circling in her chest where it felt like a knife impaled her.

"Tell me everything that happened."

He pulled up the sheriff's contact, and placed the call on speaker, informing Justice as soon as she answered.

Brielle gathered a fistful of covers and ran her finger along the seam, reminding herself to breathe as she gently rocked back and forth.

"First and foremost, I'd like to offer my sincerest condolences." The sheriff paused and all of this felt like it was happening in slow motion. "My accident investigator is on the scene and I expect an update from her on her initial findings in the next fifteen minutes. What I can tell you confidently is that your vehicle ran off the road at a high rate of speed on the highway. It careened off the highway and the driver was pronounced dead on the scene. The victim was positively identified, and her family has been notified. Again, I couldn't be sorrier."

"Thank you." Those were the only two words Brielle could manage.

Dalton reached over and covered her hand with his. There was something comforting about the move, like it was the most natural thing.

"How did the victim come to be in possession of your vehicle?"

"Gabbie borrowed my car." The word, victim, was too awful and too generic. Brielle wanted to say her name. Gabbie was a person, and Brielle wanted to be reminded of the fact. This wasn't a case to her. This was personal.

She tamped down the fear that someone could be targeting her for murder. Her mind tried to argue against it and she supposed it was some form of primal protection. Like her brain couldn't handle the fact someone wanted her dead.

After this morning's event and now this...what other conclusion could she draw?

"The driver had your permission to be in the vehicle?" It was more statement than question, like she was replaying the fact.

"Yes," Brielle answered anyway. She wanted to be very clear Gabbie hadn't stolen the car or gone for a joyride. "She was on her way to the airport to go to Dallas to meet her boyfriend. Her car wouldn't start. She's been having car trouble, and she was saving up for a new one."

A sob escaped. Brielle coughed, trying to cover but it was too late. Her body trembled. Dalton repositioned, moving beside her. He wrapped an arm around her and she burrowed into his chest.

"I'd like to stop by and take your statement," Justice said.

"I'm not going anywhere." She didn't feel the need to point out the fact she no longer had transportation. It struck her in that moment that she needed to call her parents. Word could spread quickly in a small town and she didn't want them hearing any of this from someone besides her.

Her phone was downstairs but she didn't want to move... couldn't move. Not while Dalton's arm was around her and she felt protected for the first time in a very long time.

"I'll be here in case you need to reach one of us," Dalton piped in.

"Thank you. I won't be long."

"Let us know when you're on your way," Dalton requested.

"Will do." The sheriff ended the call.

"I'm sorry about your friend," Dalton said.

The worse part about it was that Gabbie was the closest thing Brielle had to a friend here in Cattle Cove, despite growing up here. Even they rarely ever talked. Don't get her wrong, if she needed a cup of sugar or to borrow Gabbie's lawnmower, no problem. But actual friends? As in someone Brielle shared her deep, dark thoughts. Nope. There was no one who fit that bill. She and her sister had been close at one time. When Bethany went off to college, though, she changed. They still talked, but it wasn't the same anymore and hadn't been in years.

Why was that? What was the reason Brielle put her head down and worked, rarely ever connecting with neighbors or coworkers? When was the last happy hour she was invited to? Or attended even if the invite did show up?

When did she stop living?

6

G abbie was dead.

Brielle couldn't wrap her mind around the fact no matter how real it was or how many times she heard the news. It was unthinkable on every level and all she wanted to do was find the bastard responsible.

Gabbie was driving Brielle's car. The only explanation for the crash was that she'd been hit or run off the road.

Brielle was supposed to be the one in the vehicle. It was supposed to be her behind the wheel.

Gabbie was innocent. She'd done nothing wrong. She was Brielle's favorite neighbor. She was spunky and fun-loving. She was also absent-minded and a self-described hot mess.

Her death was Brielle's fault.

The mattress dipped underneath Dalton's weight as he repositioned, then stood. Glancing at the clock, Brielle realized she'd slept less than an hour. It was good enough. She pushed to standing as Dalton rounded the bed. Putting weight on her right side wasn't working out so well and she almost fell backward.

Dalton closed the distance between them in a couple of strides and grabbed hold of her arm, helping her to stay steady. So, she didn't debate her next actions when he stepped in front of her. She pushed up on her tiptoes and kissed him.

She heard his sharp intake of air and half figured he was about to tell her that she crossed a line. She had. Not just crossed but breached, destroyed, and annihilated it in one fell swoop. That was the thing about lines. She'd never liked them. Not even as a kid. And it was pure emotion taking over at this point, taking her deepest desire and not caring about the consequences.

Dalton's full lips were tender against hers as they moved slowly at first. She brought both hands up to tunnel in his thick mane. The move caused her breasts to press into his solid-walled chest and her stomach to freefall like she'd gone cliff diving. And all she wanted to do was get lost in the kiss. In his arms. In his bed.

And what would that do? The realization Dalton McGannon would only break her heart was a bucket of ice water.

"Sorry." She pulled back the second reasoning returned.

"Don't be. We just shouldn't let that happen again."

"Agreed." She felt the need to explain. "It was an in-the-moment thing. I just needed to grab onto something or someone to root me in reality again."

"Understood." His voice was gruff as he helped her downstairs and back into the kitchen.

"There's probably not a lot in the fridge since I travel so much but I can probably whip up something if you're hungry." She needed to change the subject and redirect her thoughts before they returned to the heat in that kiss against the softness of his lips.

He helped her ease onto a chair at the kitchen table.

"You have delivery here in town, right?"

"Yes."

"Do you still like pineapple and Canadian bacon on your pizza?"

"I sure do." It warmed her heart that he remembered those little details, thinking how nice it was to have history with someone. She didn't personally know anyone she worked with beyond a happy hour level.

"Then, it's my treat."

She thanked him and reached for her laptop. Her hand trembled. *Deep breath.* Her inbox was still up, and even more e-mails had hit her inbox. She wasn't in the mood, so she closed that window and opened a new tab.

After locating the website for DOUGH, she turned the screen toward Dalton. He palmed his cell and then made the call.

Outside, she saw one of her other neighbors pull into the parking pad between their houses. Brielle forced herself to stand. "I'll be right back."

Dalton started toward the door but she put her hand up to stop him. "If my neighbor sees you, she might not be as willing to talk to me. You can be a bit...distracting." It was the best word she could think of at the moment. Women could barely tear their gazes away from him and men seemed to size him up for a fight. It had always been that way, even in school, and he probably never really noticed it. She wanted Mrs. Ramshaw to be able to concentrate on the conversation.

Pushing past the pain in her right hip—pain that would be temporary for her—she moved out the backdoor and through the porch. She thought about Gabbie again and nearly burst into tears. Taking in a few calming breaths, Brielle called out to her next-door neighbor.

Mrs. Ramshaw stepped in front of her minivan, a concerned look on her face. She wore a long-sleeve cotton shirt year-round, mom jeans, and usually some type of hat. Today's was a floppy sunhat that was probably more appropriate for the beach. She waved when she saw Brielle.

"I just wanted to let you know that I'm going to have a security system installed at my house. I had a scary run-in this morning and I'm still shaken up by it."

"Oh?" Mrs. Ramshaw's kids started emptying out of the minivan. There were five in total, ranging in age from fourteen years old to two. The oldest wrangled the others. "Hannah, would you mind taking the others inside and getting them started on their craft projects?"

"Yes, Mother," the girl said with just enough boredom to know she was a teenager.

As soon as the door closed, Mrs. Ramshaw turned her attention on Brielle. "Are you okay? What happened?"

"I am now. A friend intervened. I just thought I'd warn you to keep your eyes open and be careful."

Mrs. Ramshaw shook her head. "It's half the reason we live here instead of Houston. I'm Kate, by the way."

"I grew up here and have never seen anything like what's been happening lately."

"I guess it's following us. Tate travels so much, I just didn't feel safe in a bigger city," she admitted. Her husband was on the road five days a week. He was home weekends-only and the kids sporting events seemed to keep them hopping.

Brielle had a quick mental debate about whether or not to share what she knew about Gabbie. Could she without losing it?

She had to. Kate needed to make sure she wasn't mistaken for Brielle. Plus, she would see Gabbie's family coming to her house to clean it out in the next few days or weeks. It was horrific and Brielle still couldn't grasp the fact Gabbie was gone.

On balance, she decided that Kate needed to know.

"There's one more thing." Telling her without busting into sobs might prove difficult despite the fact that Brielle was so not a crier. "It's about Gabbie."

"Oh? Did something happen?"

Deep breaths.

Brielle nodded. "I'm afraid Gabbie was in a car..."

White-hot tears burned the backs of her eyes. She ducked, chin to chest, to hide the onslaught.

"Oh, no. Is she...did she...?"

All Brielle could do was shake her head.

"That's terrible news, Brielle. I'm so sorry for her family. This must be awful for them." She stared at Brielle for a long moment. "You two got along well, didn't you?"

Brielle nodded, words escaped her.

"I'm really sorry." There was so much compassion in those words they threatened to break the dam that was barely holding back Brielle's emotions.

"Thank you." She managed to get those words out. A few more came. "Be careful."

"I appreciate the warning. I do. I'm beginning to think this isn't the town I once believed it was. I'll talk to Tate this weekend about a possible alarm. And I'll start locking the doors. Although, I generally do that anyway considering we're alone so much of the time and it's a habit from Houston." Kate shrugged like she could somehow rid herself of the bad news. "You travel a lot, don't you?" She seemed to catch herself. "It's not any of my business if you don't want to share, it's just I—"

Brielle put a hand up, palm out. "It's okay. I do. I'm gone during the week and I sometimes go see my parents on the weekends. Lately, I've been working almost non-stop. We added a few new territories and I've been going around and helping set up offices."

"I hope they gave you a promotion. And a good raise," Kate said. When it came time to negotiate for a raise, Brielle figured having Kate on her side would be a good thing. Maybe she could add her to the next performance review meeting. It couldn't hurt to have an advocate on her side and Kate was more astute than Brielle had given her credit. But then, she couldn't say that she knew the woman very well and, she was learning, outside appearances didn't always tell the whole story.

"I'll be sure to tell my boss." Brielle smiled despite her somber mood. There was something refreshingly honest about her neighbor and Brielle regretted not spending more time getting to know the woman. Of course, anyone who had five kids had to be busy dusk to dawn. There'd only been Brielle and her sister in their family. Two perfect daughters. She'd overheard her father mentioning more than once that he wanted to keep trying until they got a boy. Her mom dodged the question better than a squirrel crossing the road in traffic.

"Do you want company?" Kate glanced at the unfamiliar truck parked in front of the house.

"I'm fine. A friend of mine from high school is over actually. He just ordered food, so I should probably get back inside. I just wanted to let you know what was going on," Brielle said.

"Thank you. I'll keep watch." Kate turned toward her

house and then stopped. She spun around. "You know what? The other night I could've sworn that I heard a noise out here. It was during the week and you would have been out of town. It was late and, let's face it, nothing ever happens out here so I chalked it up to being a raccoon in the trash. When I got up the next morning to run the kids to school, sure enough, your trashcan had been turned over. I figured the animal was looking for food, so I swept it up for you and pushed the trashcan against your house. I started to leave a note but didn't want to sound like a jerk. 'Hey, your trash was turned over.' I thought it might come across like it bothered me or something. It didn't. It was easy enough to clean up and I didn't mind. That's the last I thought of it until now. Now, I'm wondering if someone was here going through your trash looking for something."

Brielle issued a sharp sigh. Who would want to go through her trash? Better yet, what did the person think he or she would find?

"Thanks for letting me know. I'll pass the information along to the sheriff. Mind if I get your number in case she wants to speak to you?" Brielle traveled and Kate had only lived next door a few mon—

Hold on.

"When did you guys move here?" she asked.

"It'll be two years ago this Christmas. We moved over the holiday break. Why?"

"I'm embarrassed that I haven't stopped by and made more of an effort to get to know you better. It feels like you moved in a couple of months ago."

"Don't worry about it. It feels like that to us too. I might even have a few boxes in the attic that I still haven't unpacked yet." Kate might be delivering a white lie, but Brielle appreciated the sentiment.

She handed over her phone. "Might be easier if you enter your contact information." Again, her hand was shaking.

Kate took the cell and entered her information. "I'm not kidding about the offer. It's open-ended. If your friend leaves and you want someone to come sit with you, just call or text. I respond to both."

The warmth in her neighbor's voice made Brielle realize she was missing out on getting to know good people literally in her own backyard.

DALTON STOOD FAR ENOUGH from the window to see what was going on outside, but not so close the neighbor could see him. Brielle turned and he felt compelled to watch as she walked toward the house. His protective instincts were on full alert. Hell, his body hummed with need as the kiss they'd shared replayed in his thoughts.

A slip in focus now could cost Brielle her life.

She opened the door as he moved to the coffee machine and made another cup. "Do you want a refresher?"

"No thanks. I did learn that someone was digging around in my trash. The person must've gotten spooked or found what they wanted and got out of here in a hurry because my neighbor said the trashcan was knocked over. She thought an animal was responsible."

Those wide hazel eyes of hers were a shot to the heart. An attraction was out of the question no matter how grown-up Brielle was now. Dalton couldn't go there with anyone. Not after what he'd lost. He could date strangers. Women who posed no risk to his heart. Because Mallory's car crash had caused him to lose two people in one freak accident. Whoa. Hold on there. Why was spending time with Brielle suddenly dredging up memories best left in the darkest corners of his mind? He'd pushed those thoughts down so deep they should never resurface. The pain still so raw that his gut twisted in a knot. And, no, he'd never told his family. Mallory's pregnancy and their plan to elope was the rare secret he kept from everyone close to him.

Dalton flexed and released his fingers a few times to ease some of his pent-up frustration. "Did she say when this happened?"

"A couple of nights ago."

The idea any of this could be random was thrown out the window.

"I'm guessing she didn't get a look at the person or people responsible," he said.

"No. She just figured it was a raccoon and then she said she cleaned up for me since she knew how much I traveled." She blinked a few times like that might wash away the nightmare for her.

"The person could have been trying to figure out if this is where you lived."

"But why? I don't have anything of value. I don't have information about anything or anyone that someone could use as blackmail. I'm honestly at a loss here. I'm an auditor for warehouses. It's not the kind of job that would put me in the line of fire if you know what I mean. I've been helping set up new offices too. So, I haven't even been doing my actual job lately."

As much as he didn't want to say this, he had to. "Women are almost always abused by someone familiar. Usually a boyfriend or significant other. Most domestic violence cases involve spouses. A woman's biggest threat is usually a person she trusts." He couldn't hide the disdain in his voice.

"I've read that too." Her shoulders deflated just a little.

"Might be time to make a list of all the people you've dated in the past six months or so. Sheriff Justice will most likely ask for one anyway. This way, you can get a head start." As much as he didn't want to see the names, she should probably write them down.

"It's not going to take long," she said and relief he had no right to own washed over him. He tried to convince himself the reason was simple. He was protective of her as a big brother figure would be. But there was nothing brotherly about his body's reaction to the kiss they'd shared or the way he felt every time he was in the same room with her.

"What about guys at your office or places you frequent? Anyone take an extra interest in you or ask you out recently? Clients?" He wouldn't rule out a stalker. Not as beautiful and magnetic as she was. She was the light and people were drawn to her. He was drawn to her.

She sucked in a burst of air and nodded.

7

"I can think of a few names now that you mention it."

Now, Dalton figured they were starting to get somewhere. Brielle had the kind of looks that got attention, wanted or not. She was sharp-minded and funny. She had the kind of laugh that would replay in his mind long after this ordeal was over and she was back on the road for work. She was easy to be around, comfortable in her own skin. If she wasn't dating, it was by choice.

He took a seat next to her and sipped his fresh brew. Her fingers danced on the keyboard after she pulled up a blank document.

"I can't begin to tell you how creepy this line of thinking is," she admitted. "The thought someone I know could be trying to hurt me."

"Focus on anyone you've turned down or anyone who is persistent," he said.

Zachary Winter
Kevin Roland
Eric Sampson
Jose Pena

Cameron…

"I can't remember his last name," she pointed out. "But he works in sales."

"You might want to underline or bold any of the ones you dated versus ones you knew from work or socially."

She highlighted one name, Eric Sampson. The doorbell rang about that time and she practically jumped out of her skin.

"I got this." Dalton figured the food had arrived. He crossed the kitchen and the living room, making it to the door as the driver lifted his fist to knock.

"Pizza delivery." The driver was young. He looked wet behind the ears. He had one of those honest faces. Was he one of the Henderson's kids?

Dalton should probably know his name. He should probably get off the ranch more. Probably, but most likely wouldn't. He pulled out cash and paid the kid, leaving a decent tip.

"Thank you." His smile was ear-to-ear.

Dalton closed and then locked the door for Brielle's benefit. The food smelled amazing. He couldn't remember the last time he'd had pizza, let alone have it show up at his door. That answer to the last part was never. And, technically, this was Brielle's place, but it had a homey feel.

And speaking of home, "Have you thought about calling your parents to let them know you're safe?"

He walked into the kitchen to find her studying her laptop.

"I've been avoiding thinking about it. But, you're right. News travels fast and I wouldn't want them hearing any of this from someone other than me." She glanced up at him. "My inbox is blowing up. I should probably make sure everything's okay at work. And that food smells incredible, by the way."

"I can grab a couple of plates if you point me in the right direction or don't mind me hunting around."

"Make yourself at home, Dalton. You're practically family as it is." The last part came out sounding a little forced. Was she trying to remind herself they had a history of friendship? Technically, he wouldn't call them friends. They got along and he thought she was a sweetheart. A four-year age difference was a big deal back then. Now, they were both adults and the gap seemed inconsequential.

Dalton moved to the cabinet she'd pointed to and pulled out a pair of plates while balancing the box in one hand. He managed to grab plates and bring everything to the table without dropping any items.

"Do you want something to drink while I'm up?"

"I can get it, Dalton."

"It's fine. I was getting a glass of water for me," he offered.

"Are you sure?" She didn't seem used to being taking care of. Not that she needed it. She was every bit capable of taking care of herself.

"Positive." He filled two glasses with water and brought them over while she dished out slices of pizza that smelled so good he was practically drooling.

"Thank you for everything you're doing for me, Dalton."

He started to wave her off like it was nothing but she stopped him.

"It's a big deal. At least, it is to me."

"I like helping you, Brielle." He left it at that, unwilling to examine the sentiment further.

"It's nice to have someone around who has my back for a change," she said.

"Are you still close with your sister?"

"Yes and no. She's moved on with Tim and now the pregnancy."

Dalton did his level best to hide his emotions at hearing those words again.

"Is it okay to talk to you about my sister?" Brielle's forehead creased with concern.

"Yes, of course. I wish her nothing but happiness."

"It's just the two of you dated and were pretty serious at one point," she said.

"As much as teenagers can be." And then it dawned on him what she was really saying. "If you're worried that I still have a thing for your sister, the answer is no."

"It's just that you gave a look and there was something in your eyes...something sad."

For a few seconds, Dalton didn't say the words on the tip of his tongue. He never talked about Mallory with anyone, not even those closest to him. Much to his utter shock, he wanted to tell Brielle. He'd been holding it inside for so long and now it felt like a boulder docked on his chest.

He took a bite of pizza and chewed on the slice.

Before he could talk himself out of it, he dove in headfirst. "I've never told a soul this before." He caught her gaze and held. "So, I'd appreciate it if you kept it between us."

"Of course," she said quickly, setting down her slice.

"Keep eating," he urged, figuring she needed the energy.

Brielle picked the slice up and did as requested. Guilt and shame cloaked him, making it hard to keep going.

"I had a girlfriend in college. More than that, if I'm honest. We talked about getting married after we graduated." He paused and closed his eyes. Recalling the memory cut like a fresh wound. "We were both juniors. Not much more than two young kids who thought they were in love. We found out she was pregnant, and I acted like a jerk."

"That doesn't seem like you."

He opened his eyes and they settled on her face, searching for...understanding? Compassion? Forgiveness?

Hell, he didn't know what he was looking for. All he could feel was an ache in his chest that made him feel like he might explode if he didn't tell someone about her.

"I was having a hard time with one of my professors. I didn't want to let my family down. I was under pressure. I was young. There are half a dozen other excuses too, but none of them matter. It was all about me when it should have been about her and the baby."

Brielle reached her free hand over and rested it on his thigh. The move was simple and yet felt incredibly intimate.

"We had a dust-up, and she took off in her car." He had to stop right there to catch his breath. He didn't need to say what had happened next, her eyes showed that she knew what he couldn't say.

"I'm so sorry, Dalton." The words were spoken soft and steady. There were other reassurances too. "No one should have to go through that. Couples argue but they work it out. Young people make mistakes." Those words were balm to a broken soul.

The next thing he knew, pizzas had been set aside and Brielle had repositioned onto his lap.

"You couldn't have known that would happen, Dalton."

"It's the *what-if*s that'll kill you," he admitted. "What if I'd reacted differently to the pregnancy? What if I'd asked her to stay instead of letting her walk out the door mad? What if I'd volunteered to go with her? What if I'd volunteered to drive? What if I'd asked her to go for a walk instead?"

She didn't comment. She just listened. And it was the best thing she could've done.

BRIELLE'S HEART bled for Dalton. She couldn't imagine the pain that would come with carrying a secret around for so long. She couldn't be certain when the air in the room changed but it went from comfort to heat in a matter of minutes. It didn't take long for her lips to find his or for him to shift her around until she faced him. Her pulse raced and her heart pounded her ribcage.

Deepening the kiss would probably be a mistake. She did it anyway. Today had been one for the books and she wanted to get lost in everything that was Dalton. If she had it her way, he'd be on top of her, pressing her into the mattress with his heft, and they'd zoom off the ledge together.

Her hip would argue differently and since her better judgment had taken flight, she figured her pain meter would keep her from going so far she couldn't return. Because that would happen with Dalton. She could lose her heart to him like she'd never lost it before. It was more than shared history. Although, she had to admit that was a bonus.

His tongue darted inside her mouth and she released the moan she'd been trying to hold back. Brielle was tired of holding back. Of only taking measured steps forward. Of valuing logic over spontaneity and stopping right before she went all-in after her heart's desire. Right now, what her heart wanted was Dalton.

So instead of pulling back enough to evaluate her next step, she brought her hands up and tunneled her fingers in his thick hair. His hands roamed free against her sensitized skin, leaving a hot trail wherever he touched. His fingers were calloused from working on the ranch and it was just about the sexiest thing. He was skilled with those hands and her stomach freefell thinking about other places she would like him to touch.

He pulled back enough to feather a hot little trail of kisses down her neck to where her pulse pounded at the base. He glanced up long enough to lock gazes for a long, slow few seconds. And his smile nearly obliterated what was left of her resolve. She wanted this. She wanted him. She wanted to let those skilled hands continue to roam her body because he was bringing to life places she never knew existed.

And it wasn't because she was inexperienced so much as she'd never been with someone who both caused a dozen butterflies to release in her chest and managed to melt her bones with one single kiss.

So, she smiled right back at him, right back into those eyes that were glittery with need and made her ache for more. And then, she closed the distance between them and brought her lips down on his with bruising need.

One of his hands roamed her back and the other cupped her full breast. Her nipple pebbled as a primal sense of urgency roared through her, bringing her body to life. There was still pain in her hip and it reminded her that she wouldn't be doing much more than kissing until it healed.

A sobering thought struck, ripping her from the haze that was Dalton. Would he still be around by the time she healed?

This time, she pulled back. Breath heaving, she could only imagine how incredible sex with Dalton would be. And that's exactly where that thought had to be shelved. For now.

He pressed his forehead against hers as they breathed in each other's breaths. She placed the flat of her palm against the center of his chest. His heart raced at the same tempo as hers.

"Confession," she started, wondering if it was a good idea to admit this. "I've never been so turned on by a simple kiss before."

"Simple?" He feigned insult and she laughed.

"Yep," she teased. It was so nice to have some of the tension broken up. Their situations were heavy and none of this was going away anytime soon. She couldn't even think about Gabbie without tearing up. But in order to find Gabbie's killer, Brielle was going to have to separate herself from her grief as best as she could in order to find the person responsible and ensure justice was served. No question. She would do whatever it took for Gabbie because she didn't deserve...

Brielle shifted gears. Giving into her emotions wouldn't help the situation and she would think more clearly if she could relax a little bit. But the playful feeling she'd felt a few seconds ago was gone.

"We should probably eat," she said.

Dalton's eyebrow went up, but he seemed to know better than to comment. Instead, he nodded as she eased from his lap and onto the chair she'd been sitting in before the kisses —kisses that would now set the standard for every other kiss for the rest of her life.

She thought about what he'd shared.

"Thank you for trusting me, Dalton," she said.

"I could say the same thing to you." He paused. "And there isn't anyone else I'd rather talk about that with, or about anything else in my past, present, and future."

Didn't those words cause her heart to freefall again?

He was making a habit of it. A habit she liked even if she didn't know what to do with her attraction to him.

"I travel all the time for work." She left it at that.

A look of something—was it hurt?—passed behind his eyes.

"My life is on the ranch. I don't leave a whole lot." His admission explained why he didn't 'do' relationships. And she figured his work was a convenient excuse to keep people at arm's length.

"And probably don't want to," she added for good measure.

"Nope. Sure don't." He picked up the unfinished piece of pizza and took another bite.

"It's a beautiful place. Why would you want to leave?" She just let that sit there, making herself abundantly clear. No response was needed.

8

Dalton's cell buzzed. He checked the screen. "The sheriff is out front. I can go call her in if you want to finish working on your list of names."

"Okay."

One-word answers weren't his favorite but what else could either one of them say? The attraction between them had a mind of its own no matter how much logic argued against it or excuses tried to quash it. The sheriff's arrival was a sobering reminder of the temporary nature of their... what? Friendship? Alliance? And what about when this was over? He'd go back to his life. She'd go back to hers. Two separate paths.

The prospect had never struck him square in the chest like it did right now.

Dalton opened the door as the sheriff took the last step onto the porch. "Come on in."

She followed him into the kitchen and the first thing she repeated to Brielle was how sorry she was for her loss.

"I've been working on a list of names for you," Brielle said. The lost look in her eyes had returned.

Anger burned through him because he wanted to be the one to ease her pain. The only thing he could offer was a temporary shelter in a raging storm. Right now, that would be his focus if she would allow it.

The sheriff walked over to the chair where Brielle sat. She repositioned the laptop screen to make it easier for Justice to see. Instead of using a notebook, she pulled out her cell phone and took a quick shot of the screen. The notebook came out next.

"Start at the top of the list and tell me what your connection is to the person and why he made the list." The sheriff moved beside Brielle and took a seat in the chair Dalton pulled out for her.

"Okay." Brielle shot an awkward glance toward Dalton. "Then, I'll start with Zachary Winter. He's a trainer at the gym I used to go to."

"Used to go to?"

"That's right. I quit a few months ago because he creeped me out. He would come into a class I would be taking and single me out to 'partner' stretch with or he always wanted to 'spot' me if I was in a weights class. He was flirty, which I ignored. But then he started following me out to my car and that got weird."

"Did you mention any of this to the manager?" the sheriff asked.

Dalton flexed and released his fingers to work off some of the tension. What he wanted most to do was find Zachary Winter and give him a few lessons on personal space.

"No. Honestly, the place was a little farther than I wanted to drive anyway. Work picked up, so I froze my membership. You know how it is with most gyms. The trainers bounce around. I figured by the time I would have a chance to work out regularly again he'd be gone anyway." She shrugged.

"Do you remember the last time you saw him or had an encounter?"

"I can check my statement for the date. I literally came home and froze the account after he tried to block me from getting inside my car one day." She moved the laptop screen out of view of the others and then her fingers danced on the keyboard. "Let me see." She studied the screen. "Looks like September twenty-second."

The sheriff asked for the name of the gym and verified the statement activity after Brielle repositioned the laptop to show the screen. Justice took down a few notes beside Winter's name. "Anything else I need to know about Mr. Winter?"

"I didn't know him very well. He started working at the gym over the summer in late June or early July."

"Okay. Tell me about Kevin Roland."

"He's a guy from work. I've been helping him set up a field office in one of our larger client locations. The two of us were assigned to work together and it's not uncommon for teams to eat meals together. Kevin would have a few beers and then he'd hit on me. I chalked it up to him having one too many after working long hours. But then we were suddenly in hotel rooms next door to each other. I checked with our admin at work and she said Kevin told her that I asked the rooms be set up that way."

"But you didn't."

"Nope. He said it was for safety reasons." She shook her head. "I confronted him about it because I wanted him to know I didn't want him to speak for me. Ever. Especially when it involved hotel rooms or travel with a colleague."

"How did he react?"

"Said he was embarrassed but that he genuinely wanted to look out for me."

Dalton almost spewed the coffee in his mouth after taking a sip. As far as excuses went, that was one for the books. If this Roland guy meant those words, he would have asked her permission to room next door.

"In your opinion, was he telling the truth?" the sheriff asked.

"I couldn't tell you one way or the other. His drinking was a problem. I asked him to stop or slow down. I stopped going to dinner with him," Brielle admitted. "It helped."

"Are you still in contact with Mr. Roland?"

"Yes. The project won't be finished for another couple of weeks." Once again, Brielle shot an awkward glance toward Dalton. "He's been texting me with questions."

"Can I take a look at those texts?"

Brielle searched around for her phone. Found it. She unlocked it and glanced at the screen, making a comment about her e-mails blowing up at work. She sighed sharply before handing over the phone.

The sheriff examined the screen and then scrolled through. Dalton was tempted to walk over there and stand over the sheriff's shoulder to get a look. He had to take a step back and fight the urge. It wasn't his place, and, besides, he was only here for support. Didn't stop him from grinding his teeth in anger, though.

"Who is next on the list?" The sheriff returned the cell to its owner. She wrote a few notes on her pad of paper.

"Eric Sampson. We dated a few weeks after meeting in a bar. Gabbie..." Her voice cracked on the name. "My friend used to like to go country dancing. She dragged me out a few times. Eric was nice at first, but he fell a little too fast. He wanted more in the relationship. I didn't. He said hurtful things. Made a few idle threats, but nothing that he has followed through on and I refused to go back to the bar where we met. Not a hardship for someone who would rather curl up and watch a movie on a Friday night than hit the clubs." Brielle's cheeks flushed with embarrassment. "I hadn't been out in a long time and he was persistent. I thought it was cute at first. He showed a lot of interest. Then, it got to be smothering. So, I cut off all contact."

"Did Mr. Sampson let it drop?"

"He sent a few texts that I deleted. I figured he needed time to let it go, so I blocked his number," she admitted.

"And did he?" The sheriff blinked. "Let it go?"

"No."

"HE SHOWED up at my work a few times, waiting in the parking lot for me. I had to get security to walk me out." Hearing the details of her negative interactions with men, dating or otherwise, made Brielle want to cringe.

"How long ago was this?"

"Again, a few months ago. I volunteered to help set up field offices for a change of pace and I figured it wouldn't hurt to be unavailable."

"When was the last time you saw or heard from him?"

"After I blocked his number and took the assignment... that was pretty much it." Brielle gave over all the personal information she had on Eric. She hadn't gone to his house, but she did know his cell number and he was on social media. The sheriff should be able to track him down easily enough.

"I'm guessing you haven't been back to the bar?"

She shook her head. "Not my scene anyway."

"Which one did you and your friend go to?"

"Boots and Spurs."

"Okay." The sheriff wrote down the name. "What about the other two names on the list? What do the italics mean?"

"These are just guys who have asked me out and didn't take my rejection very well. Jose works in the executive office and Cameron is from sales. He's the pushy one. You know, a guy who thinks he can talk his way into or out of any situation."

Sheriff Justice nodded.

"And, as I said, Jose works in the executive offices. He's quiet but I get the feeling he doesn't take rejection well. A rumor started about me being an ice queen not long after I turned him down and I'm almost positive he had something to do with it."

The longer Brielle talked, the more tension she felt radiating from Dalton over in the corner. He stood there, leaning his hip against the counter, taking it all in. He would definitely be classified as more of the quiet type, except there was nothing backhanded about him. He was trustworthy, true to his word, and a person could never have a better ally.

Brielle took in a deep breath.

"Sounds like he held a grudge. Did he ever do anything similar to anyone else at the office?" Sheriff Justice asked.

"We didn't work on the same floor, so I have no idea. Plus, I'm rarely in the office. I did hear something a while back about him dating his administrative assistant."

Sheriff Justice nodded, taking down more notes. "Anyone else who might be holding a grudge? Someone you've recently had a dispute with?"

"I work so much of the time. I pay my taxes and pretty much live and let live. As far as I know, no one should hold anything against me. I don't try to cheat anyone or pick up married men." She didn't try to pick up any men, to be honest, but this didn't seem like the right time to point it out. She didn't have many girlfriends and only occasionally went out with Gabbie. "I keep my opinions to myself. There are no fights or drama other than what I've told you, and I promise you that I didn't invite those into my life." All of which occurred in the past four or five months.

The sheriff looked up from her notepad. "Anything else you can think of that I might need to know?"

Brielle shook her head. She literally drew a blank.

"If anything comes to you, you already have my number." The sheriff stood up.

"Yes, ma'am." She snapped her fingers. "As a matter of fact, it was an SUV that cut me off the night I fell asleep at the wheel. That's all I remember. It was dark but I couldn't tell you if it was black or dark blue. I was so shocked that I'd actually nodded off."

"Okay. And the plates?"

"Nothing there." Brielle shook her head.

"I can see myself out." She excused herself. Dalton followed to lock the front door, something Brielle was certain wasn't a habit for him. She appreciated the extra effort to make her feel safe.

Given there'd been two incidences spaced hours apart, it was clear someone was targeting her. Didn't an icy chill run down her spine when she let the thought take seed?

She remembered to call her parents. She picked up her phone and hit the contact, realizing that her hands were still trembling just a little bit.

Steadying her voice as best as she could, she said, "First things first, Dad. I'm fine."

"No good conversation ever started with that sentence,"

he mused. Her dad was one of the sweetest people on earth. Her parents were older when she and her sister were born and they'd long since retired.

"I had an incident this morning when riding my bike and now a friend of mine was run off the road in my car. Sheriff Justice is on the case and Dalton McGannon is here with me now." She rushed the words out for fear she might chicken out or sob. Neither would be good for the conversation she needed to have with her folks. She didn't want to sound the alarm. If someone truly was after her, the last thing she wanted to do was bring them to her parents' house. A thought struck. Would the person go after them anyway?

No. No. No.

She couldn't let herself go down that road. The path that made her worry that everyone close to her would end up a target.

Dalton walked back into the room and cleared the table. She felt his presence in the room before he so much as made a noise. Bandit sat by the door and there was so much comfort having him in the room.

"Brielle? Are you still there?"

"Yes, Dad."

"Did you hear my question? Because you didn't answer."

"Sorry. What was the question again? I zoned out there for a second."

"Do you want me and your mother to come stay with you? I can bring the shotgun." It was sweet of her father to want to protect her, but she couldn't agree to it.

"No. Thanks, Dad. I'll be fine. The sheriff is on the case. I'm not alone. At least for now. My next-door neighbor told me to stop by any time if I get scared or need someone to talk to." She had no idea how long Dalton planned to stay but saw him nodding out of the corner of her eye. From a place deep in her heart she hoped he'd stick around despite the confusing feelings his presence stirred in her chest.

She was clear on wanting him. The confusion came with how much she felt like she needed him in such a short time. Not to complete her. She was a whole person already. But to compliment her, to give her a confidant and someone she couldn't wait to race home to every night.

"Are you sure? Or we could grab that rental house in Ruidoso where we used to go in the summers." His suggestion was sweet and brought back a flood of happy memories. But hiding didn't seem like the right play. It might drag this out even longer and she was already so done. She wasn't stupid, though. And if the sheriff or Dalton thought it was a good idea to lie low for a while, of course she would seriously consider the request.

"I'm a hundred percent, Dad. Thank you, though."

"Do you want me to tell your mother?"

"Only in a way that won't cause her to worry and definitely before someone else does. I don't want her getting the wrong idea." Brielle's mother had always been closer to Bethany, and, to be honest, distanced from Brielle, who was her dad's favorite. Her parents still had a couple of friends in town. The sheriff would be asking around. Dots would be connected, especially with Dana having seen what happened this morning.

"Sweetheart, are you in some kind of trouble?"

"Nothing I can't handle, Dad." She really hoped the statement was true. "I have to go, though. Like I said, Dalton is here, and I don't want to be rude by staying on the phone the whole time.

"Okay then. Be safe and know that we love you."

"I love you guys too, Dad." She ended the call and then set the phone down on the table.

Dalton started pacing and his brow was furrowed like he was concentrating on solving a complicated math equation.

"He's a coward."

9

"Excuse me?"

Dalton realized he'd offended Brielle and he immediately understood why. He'd been lost in his thoughts whereas she'd been talking to her father "I wasn't talking about your dad. He's one of the nicest people you'd ever meet."

That seemed to clarify where he was going with this.

"But this person, think about it. He tried to run over you while you were on a bike and then he literally ran your car off the road. He's hiding behind his vehicle." They were making an assumption here that they were dealing with a male. Statistically speaking and because of her previous interactions, a male was more probable.

Brielle's face muscles twitched at the revelation. "Which means he doesn't want to be seen."

"Exactly. The sheriff is probably already onto this line of thinking but maybe we can help her get to the finish line faster." He made another lap around the cozy space. "If I'm right, he won't come at you head on."

"He's been trying to make it look like a hit and run," she said. "Both times."

"There are a lot of reasons why he wouldn't want to show his face. For one, you could recognize him." Dalton's money had been on the perp being someone close to her, someone she knew. Was he someone she'd welcome into her house if he stopped by?

"If I'm dead, I don't see how that would matter. It's not like I can testify if I'm six feet under." A shiver rocked her body.

"Can I get something for you? A blanket?"

"I'm fine."

He wasn't falling into that trap. "I don't mind getting something for you. Didn't I pass a blanket on the couch in the next room?"

She nodded and smiled, so he didn't wait for her to respond. Besides, he was just pacing anyway. Moving always helped him think better when he got stuck. He brought the light blanket to her and wrapped it around her shoulders.

"I'm probably being naïve here, but it's impossible for me to think someone I know would try to hurt me. Let alone kill me. I've been so busy at work recently that I promise I haven't done anything to make someone mad."

"The incident at the gym happened a little while ago. It did strike me that it would be odd if he waited until now to retaliate, but then again, we don't know what's going on in his life. Something might have happened or a series of events that kicked off at the time you turned him down." He was just spitballing here, but he'd heard about mental triggers and how they could activate certain parts of the brain.

"This kind of crime always has to have a reason behind them, right? To be clear, we're talking about attempted murder and murder...Gabbie's. Jose is the one I trust the least because he seemed so underhanded about getting back at me."

"Starting a rumor is pretty cowardly if you ask me." Bandit stirred and she reached down to pet him. Dalton liked how well she connected with his dog. "If we approach this the same way Justice is, we're looking for means, motive, and opportunity. The perp has tried to use his vehicle twice now. It seems like his preferred MO."

"Kevin from the gym drove a Mustang. I know this because he used to park next to my car, so I'd have to pass by him in the lot."

Didn't rule the gym rat out but didn't point a finger at him either. Dalton didn't bother to hide the fact he'd fisted his right hand. Hearing about the guy made Dalton wish he had a punching bag close by.

"And neither did Eric. He drove a sports car," she clarified. "I have no idea what Zachary, Jose, or Cameron drive."

"Didn't you and Zachary drive to dinner together?" he asked.

"Yes. But we had rental cars and sometimes used a service."

"Would it help to swing by the office to check?" Zachary sounded like a real piece of work. He'd displayed passive-aggressive behavior by going behind her back to make arrangements with the administrative assistant for their department.

"The building is undergoing some kind of security system overhaul. We all got a notice about it and that's the reason I'm working from home this week."

"Is everyone else doing the same as you?"

"I guess so. Everyone who can. Some jobs require special software or access to a computer system that makes it impossible to work from home. A few departments are exempt just by the nature of their function. Maintenance, for instance, can't exactly telecommute."

"When was the last time you went to the office?" He was curious because he'd been locked onto the perp being a stalker or someone she'd rejected. Since she didn't get out much by her own admission, he'd been focused on a very close circle of people. Basically, people within a stone's toss of her.

Was that the right move?

Since Dalton didn't have a better plan, he decided to stick with the one he knew. At the very least, they had a starting point and could start crossing off names from there.

"Someone at your job would know you were working from home," he pointed out.

"And possibly hang around town to see if I showed up somewhere?" she asked.

"It's a stretch. I know. I'm just looking at your inner circle to see if we can find an answer there. Doesn't mean we're on the right track."

"My head is starting to spin from overthinking this. I'd ask if we could take Bandit for a walk, but I'm afraid to step outside."

"I don't blame you."

"I'm being a coward."

"You're being smart. There's a difference when someone is threatening your life." He resisted the urge to walk over to her and touch her. It was so tempting. It would be so easy to walk right over to her and be her comfort. It could ignite a flame that, at the moment, was a slow burn. As evidenced by earlier, it wouldn't take much of a spark to ignite a blaze. As much as he didn't want to get inside his head about the impact Brielle was having on his heart, he couldn't ignore the pain that would come with separating again. He'd gotten by okay on his own. Hadn't he?

Dalton had Bandit. He was a great companion. Well, Dalton really was getting punchy now. He'd just basically equated his dog with the best company he'd had in years. Sadly, until Brielle, it was probably true.

The reason was solid. He'd lost a lot. He'd kept the pain inside. He'd done a number on himself in the process. But regrets were about as productive as pouring gasoline on a cornfield instead of water and expecting a crop. All he'd get, with the right spark, was an all-consuming blaze. Since that was about as appealing as chasing a ghost pepper with a shot of tequila, he decided a long time ago that he didn't do regret. Anger...now that was an emotion. One that had reminded him that he was alive after losing Mallory and the kid he never knew he wanted until they were both gone.

Wasn't that the very definition of irony?

"EVERYTHING OKAY?" Brielle noticed a shift in Dalton's mood, and she couldn't help but wonder if he was still thinking about the case or was it something else altogether? It was like a sudden cold chill had entered the room, going from July to February in a matter of seconds.

Was he thinking about the baby he'd lost? Or the person he'd considered spending the rest of his life with? Either way, the mood had changed.

And now she was overthinking and couldn't help but feel like they were missing something. Don't get her wrong, she understood the reasoning behind the route they'd chosen to go down. She'd heard time and time again that women were most threatened by the men in their lives—

men they knew intimately and trusted. She'd seen a side to some men in her years of dating that caused her to believe the possibility existed.

"All things considered."

"I'm not sure what your plans are, but I would love for you to stay over tonight. My brain is seriously cramping and probably won't give me what I want until I stop thinking about the case so hard. You know?"

"I do. The more you focus on something the further it gets away from you."

"Exactly." She nodded and smiled just a little.

"I saw a big screen TV in the living room. Do you have satellite? Or cable? Or whatever it is you have available here?" He smiled.

She laughed. No, he probably wouldn't know much about how TVs worked inside town. "I have a streaming service."

"Well then, I'll stay. Just need to run out to the truck at some point and grab Bandit's emergency food."

"Are you always this prepared?" Did she really want to know the answer to the question? Because it meant he had enough sleepovers to warrant an overnight kit.

"A rancher isn't that much different than a Boy Scout. We're always prepared. I never know when I might get a call to run off poachers or if one of my brothers needs me. I always keep fresh clothes in case I have to make an unexpected trip out of town. Don't even get me started on the weather that sometimes blows through. When I'm out on the land, I don't always have time to run all the way back to my place."

"Oh." Made total sense when she heard it put that way. Of course, he would be ready for almost anything. He probably ran into weather systems and dangers more than he cared to. So, she felt a little bit silly for snapping to the obvious reason a guy as seriously hot as Dalton would have a 'sleepover' bag on the ready.

"Do you want me to help you walk?" His eyebrows drew together in concern and, man, was it incredible to have someone around who cared about her. Having her parents and sister was great, but they had their own lives. And, although, any one of them would drop what they were doing in a heartbeat to come help if she needed it, she didn't want to pull them away from their lives. She'd grown up. Her sister had grown up. Everyone had moved on and she'd become accustomed to being a party of one.

"That would be nice actually."

Dalton held out his arm and she used it like a metal bar to pull herself up. The hip raged. The only thing that hurt less than walking was sitting. So that was cool.

"What do you think about swinging by the ER to get an X-ray on that hip?" Dalton asked.

"I promise it's just a bad bruise. It'll start feeling better tomorrow." She hoped so. This pain was on the real side, and she figured Dalton wouldn't give up until she got it checked out if it didn't start improving. She wouldn't be stupid about it.

"Okay." Slow and steady, they made progress into the living room.

"From chair to chair. Not sure if I can handle this work-out," she teased. Her brain was basically mush at this point. It had been an emotionally exhausting day. Giving into the sadness trying to overtake and drag her under her might make her miss something important in Gabbie's case. Brielle couldn't let that happen. She had to dig deep and pull from a well of strength to keep a clear mind.

"Next thing you know, you'll be signing up for CrossFit if

you keep up this level of activity." He helped her ease onto the couch, positioning on her left side.

"Who knows, maybe I'll qualify for a job in the barn at your family's ranch."

"Now there's an idea." He sized her up and heat trailed everywhere his gaze traveled. "Let me see those arm muscles again?"

She flexed and they both laughed. It was so easy to be with Dalton. Even as a shy kid, she'd come out of her shell a little more when he was around. He had the kind of easy way about him that made everyone relax. The sensation was strange because he was also so ridiculously hot that her stomach felt like it was cliff diving when he locked gazes and don't even get her started about the butterflies in her chest. Dalton might be easy on the eyes, but he had the power to be hard on the heart.

"I'll run out to my truck and be right back. Are you good here for a few minutes?" As though on cue, Bandit waltzed into the room, hopped on the couch next to her and curled up.

"Looks like my protector has arrived."

The look on Dalton's face lit a thousand little campfires inside her. So, yeah, great job on keeping her attraction under control.

He didn't say anything as he turned and headed toward the door. Bandit didn't budge, so she gave him a good scratch in that spot behind the ears that got the big dog's leg moving.

"Does that feel good?" Brielle reached across the dog's body for the remote on the side table. He pawed at her arm as it stretched over him. "Oh, you want more, do you? You do realize that I'm not a professional masseuse. Right?"

Apparently not. He stared up at her with the biggest set of honey-brown eyes she'd ever seen.

"Oh, you're good." She relented, petting him with one hand while wrangling the remote with the other one. She managed to get a menu up by the time Dalton came back inside the house.

He took a couple of steps into the room before catching himself. He circled back and then locked the door. "Old habits die hard."

She couldn't help but wonder what all that statement covered. His habit of walking away from women? It was the guess she made after he shared his personal tragedy with her and how it had affected him.

Understandable. Also, a shame on all fronts.

Brielle could only imagine what it would be like to lose someone so close to her. Both of her parents were still alive. Her sister was in good health and expecting a baby. A baby. Her heart took a dive.

Hold on there one second. Brielle was happy for her sister beyond belief. But when did she start getting gooey over babies? They could be cute. Don't get her wrong. They just looked like a whole lot of work.

Bandit here was the best of both worlds. He was adorable. He seemed super comfortable being right by her side. He was no work at all.

A dog was just Brielle's speed.

She scanned the list of movies, wondering if he still liked those action-adventure flicks. If it involved chasing a mummy, or had a man with the first name Indiana, Dalton was all-in.

There were quite a few to choose from and she realized how little she actually watched TV. Maybe she could slow down and get into movies. Get a dog?

"Don't worry, Bandit. No one can replace you."

He wagged his tail the minute he heard his name, and it swished against her arm. She thought about going back to work next week, back in the field. She had no idea how long it would be before the security system at the main campus would be up and running again. She'd successfully avoided checking her e-mails today and, for the first time in a long time, it felt good to unplug.

There was a sense of relief in not having her cell glued to her hand so much. It was a large part of the reason she didn't watch TV anymore. The last thing she wanted to do after looking at a screen all day was to look at another screen.

Before Zachary, she'd hit the gym as often as she could. Her job meant she sat in an office, alone most of the time, and double-checked company records. She occasionally had to check physical inventory to make sure the numbers matched up. Therein lay the reason she had to be onsite. But computers did the heavy lifting.

TV was nice. Helped her unplug from that work mindset at the end of the day.

Dalton walked into the room. Worry lines creased his forehead. He held out a cell phone flat out on his palm.

"Your cell keeps buzzing. Thought you might want to check. I glanced over at it and the name you mentioned earlier rolled onto the screen. The heavy drinker from your office."

"Kevin?"

10

Dalton stood in the living room after handing over Brielle's phone, waiting for the big revelation that had her creepy coworker texting her. A jealous streak a mile long ripped through Dalton and since that was as productive as driving a vehicle without any gas, he shoved it aside.

Brielle stared at the screen for a long moment after scrolling, and he was pretty certain all the blood drained from her face.

"What is it?"

She blinked up at him.

"Kevin's texts led me to check my inbox, which has been flooded with e-mails." The look of shock and disbelief on her face reminded him so much of how she looked this morning, which seemed like a lifetime ago at this point. "There was an accident at the office, and someone died."

"What kind of accident?"

"Let me check." She continued scrolling. "I guess this was the reason my phone was blowing up with e-mails and the chat for employees. Corporate communications has been issuing updates and people have been responding. Kevin's text was asking me if I knew her and could believe what happened."

Dalton just bet that Kevin was solely interested in Brielle's feelings at this point. Did he expect her to be shaken up? Did he want to be her shoulder to lean on?

And why did both of those questions hit Dalton like a physical punch? He'd already overreacted to Brielle and Joel seeming chummy this morning. So, basically, he was starting to lose it. Brielle was an adult. She had male coworkers, friends, and acquaintances. This news shouldn't shock or rattle him, especially in light of the bigger picture here.

"Do you know the person?" he asked.

Brielle shook her head. "Her name is Sophie Freedland." She studied the screen, squinting her eyes at the electronic device. "She doesn't work on my floor. She's in legal."

"Does it say what happened?" Dalton fished his cell out of his pocket, figuring a story like this would make news, especially if it involved a prominent member of the community.

"Just that the incident occurred in the elevator shaft."

"Didn't you say the company is having everyone work from home right now?" Dalton remembered her words explicitly.

"Yes. But it's voluntary. We can go in if we need to and I can imagine she would have sensitive information on her computer at work. It's possible that she doesn't have the kind of job that really allows her to work from home. We're a decent-sized company with multiple divisions. I work in the warehouse auditing side." She flashed eyes at him. "You already know that, though."

He nodded.

"This is so sad. She leaves behind a husband and a kid, Dalton."

"That is terrible," he agreed. Old feelings—feelings he'd tucked away deep—resurfaced. He knew what it was like to lose a future. A piece of him wanted to reach out to the woman's husband. It was horrific to be so close to someone and then lose them so suddenly. There'd been no warning for him, either. No time to prepare for the worst. One minute he had everything he could want, even if the timing was all wrong and he wasn't one hundred percent on board yet, and the next he had nothing. He'd made it through junior year, then senior. Barely. School had been a distraction, giving him time to tuck his feelings down deep. And then by the time he graduated and came home, no one was the wiser.

Granted, Dalton's child never made it into the world, but he'd wondered what life would have been like if he or she had, more times than he cared to admit. His relationship with the child's mother wasn't perfect. He could have made it work, though. He would have made it work for the child's sake. No kid deserved to be brought into the world into an environment they were viewed as an inconvenience.

Dalton would have gotten there emotionally. He would have rallied. Granted, he didn't have the same feelings for Mallory, but he'd loved her in his own way. Their relationship had been puppy love cut short. He believed he could have gotten there with her, though, given enough time.

He gave himself a mental shake to break free from the fog.

When he looked up at Brielle, she was studying him.

"Are you okay?"

"Fine."

"You don't have to talk to me, Dalton." He felt the wall

trying to come up between them despite her efforts to fight against it. "But I'm here. And I don't just mean today. I'm talking about tomorrow and the next day. Your friendship is important to me and I'd like to be there for you if you'll allow it."

Dalton thought long and hard about whether he wanted to keep his mouth shut or not. He'd been doing just that for more years than he cared to count now. And he was doing fine...right?

So, why was he questioning his survival tactic? Because there were times...they didn't happen very often...but there were times when he felt an ache so deep it threatened to drag him under the surface of the water and toss him around until he didn't know up from down anymore.

And, yet, holding it in all these years hadn't done anything to ease his pain.

He issued a sharp sigh. "It reminds me of everything I lost, and I feel for the guy."

"Oh, Dalton. I'm so sorry. No one should have to go through what you did," she soothed.

"I'm not looking for pity." He wasn't sure what he was searching for. A way out of the guilt? A way for the ache to stop? For the hole in his chest to be filled again?

"And you won't get it from me. All I mean is that I've never met anyone as brave as you. Most people would break under similar circumstances. And yet, here you are. Still standing. Still helping someone else. You're amazing and I have a whole new respect after seeing your strength."

Funny. Those were the same words he would use to describe her.

"Thank you." Those two words had been hard to find but he'd never meant them more. "We were young and I'm not even certain the relationship would have worked."

"Doesn't matter. That's almost worse. It must feel...I'm not sure if this is the right word but the one that comes to mind is *unfinished*."

"That's a good word." It was true on so many levels. Mallory's death made it impossible to ask for forgiveness or make it right with her after he'd acted like a jerk. "I was selfish."

"You were young. I have yet to meet a twenty-year-old Mother Teresa. It's the nature of the age. Don't you think?"

He'd been too busy condemning his own actions to think about the situation logically. In hindsight, he could admit that he'd been hard on himself. "She didn't deserve to die."

"No."

"Her parents didn't deserve to lose a daughter and a grandchild in one fell swoop."

"No."

"She was too young, too vibrant." The lifeless image of her in the casket haunted him to this day.

"It's not fair."

"She deserved to live."

"There's no question about that, Dalton." She paused for a long moment. "But so do you."

Before he could form an argument, her hand came up to stop him from speaking.

"Hear me out. Okay?" She waited for his response.

He thought about it for a minute before relenting. "Go ahead."

"How many years are you going to punish yourself for something that was outside your control?"

Again, he started to form an argument, but she stopped him.

"Mallory didn't deserve to lose her life or her child. No

question there. But neither did you. You lost someone you loved. And no matter how many years you punish yourself for letting her walk out the door while she wasn't in the right frame of mind to drive, you can't bring her back." She stopped like she was letting that sink in before she added, "If she loved you as much as I believe she did, she would want you to be happy."

Those words were a mallet to his casing around his chest. He'd never turned the situation around and thought about it from Mallory's perspective. Although he wasn't ready to let himself off the hook for her death, Brielle gave him a new perspective to chew on.

"Thank you," was all he said. All he wanted to say.

And then he leaned in and feathered a kiss against her lips.

DALTON'S KISS was so tender it robbed Brielle's breath.

He pulled back and rested his forehead against hers. Neither spoke nor seemed to feel the need to. This was the most intimate moment she'd ever experienced whilst fully dressed.

Bandit seemed to approve, considering his tail had basically become a fan.

The e-mail from work about one of the employees being involved in an accident at work kept bouncing through her thoughts. Her cell dinged again, indicating another e-mail was coming in. She needed to turn off notifications.

Hold on a second. When was Sophie's accident?

She broke the moment happening between them to check her phone.

"What is it? What's going on?" Dalton asked.

"A thought just occurred to me. I was in the office a couple of nights ago. I stopped off before coming home after a long drive. I was tired." She checked the date of the accident. "I was there."

She'd been in the office on the same night. Distracted. Could it have been her falling down the broken elevator shaft instead of Sophie Freedland?

"Did the two of you cross paths?"

"I mean, I didn't think so before. Now, I'm not so certain." It was the sort of coincidence that made a cold chill raced up her spine. "I don't have a lot of interaction with anyone from legal, so I could pass her in the street and not realize it."

Dalton pulled his cell out of his pocket and palmed it. He pulled up the internet browser. He scrolled. "I don't see anything here. No news story about the accident. No obituary."

"Maybe in a couple of days. Her husband must be reeling from the news and it looks like their daughter is young. He's probably got his hands full trying to comfort and care for her." She was making a lot of assumptions, but they seemed logical.

Dalton looked like he was about to say something and then thought better of it. He closed the browser, locked the screen, and then set his phone on the coffee table, face down. "You've had enough to think about for one day." Palms up, he put his hands in the surrender position. "No more phone for me. What do you say? Join me?"

He was right. They'd had enough tragedy for one day. She hit the button to turn her phone off. Then, she set it down next to his.

"I'm in."

He rewarded her with a smile that was all Dalton, devastation that hinted at more than a little trouble.

"What did you find for us and where's the popcorn?" he asked.

She smiled back at him and some of the heavy weight she'd been feeling lifted. It amazed her what the simple act of smiling could do for her mood. It was such a small act on the surface that required very little muscle control. And yet, the effect it had on her mindset was astonishing.

Brielle reminded herself to smile more once this was all over.

"Tomb Mummy looks promising."

His eyes lit up. She nailed it.

"I like it."

"And the popcorn is in the cupboard." She nodded toward the kitchen. "Drinks in the fridge."

"I can't remember the last time I drank Coke."

"This is your lucky day," she said.

"For more than just that reason," he said low and under his breath as he walked out of the room.

Bandit's tail worked double time and for a half second, she wondered if the dog understood words. Then again, maybe all he knew were intentions.

Brielle palmed the remote and pulled up the movie. The minute she heard the microwave ding, she put her finger on the OK button. Dalton came in with a TV tray hooked onto his arm. He set up their movie night in a few minutes, settled into the spot next to her, and flashed that white-toothed smile.

"Ready?" he asked, and her stomach gave a little flip.

The word, *No*, came to mind because she would never be ready for the devastation that was Dalton. But she said, "Yes," then clicked the button and settled in.

Watching the movie was exactly the distraction she needed. It broke up some of the tension from the day. Having Dalton by her side was something she could get used to but reminded herself not to get too comfortable.

When the credits rolled, Dalton pushed to standing. Without saying a word, he cleaned up. He called Bandit into the kitchen. A few minutes later, she heard the back door open and close. The urge to get up and check to make sure he'd remembered to lock the door was strong. Instead of acting on it, she reminded herself to breathe. To really breathe.

Bandit came into the room, tail wagging. Dalton strolled in a few seconds later.

"Are you tired?" he asked.

"My eyelids are heavy but I doubt I could sleep." She pushed to standing. "You know what sounds good? A shower. Pajamas."

He looked like he bit his tongue rather than say what popped into his mind. "Not a good idea to put the image of you in the shower in my mind."

Her first instinct was to ask him to join her. She wasn't that bold even though her brain tried to reason that he wasn't exactly a stranger or a one-night stand, which was exactly the problem. He was neither and it was already going to hurt bad enough when he went back to the ranch.

"Need help?" He laughed when he seemed to hear how that sounded. "Getting up the stairs, I mean."

"Resting it has helped a lot. I think I can manage." She didn't want to admit that she was still a little freaked out by the day's events. "Any chance you'd be willing to come upstairs with me anyway? It's been a long—"

He waved her off like it was no big deal and completely unnecessary for her to finish her sentence.

That was the thing she was starting to realize about being with someone she had history with. He knew her almost as well as she knew herself. They'd been friends first. Technically not friends, since he'd been in a relationship with her sister, but still close.

Back then, her feelings were nothing more than a crush on an older guy. At that time, their age difference would have been a big deal. Dalton never gave her a second glance. In fact, she wouldn't have known him at all if it hadn't been for her sister. Now, four years seemed like nothing.

And speaking of Bethany, she probably wouldn't love the idea Brielle was spending so much time with the ex who'd broken her heart.

11

Dalton stayed a step behind Brielle, ready to catch her if she took a tumble. She was managing, though, too stubborn to accept help. Her spunk was one on a long list of qualities he admired in her.

It was impossible not to compare the two sisters. Where Brielle was fire and spunk, her sister had been placid. The term what-you-see-is-what-you-get came to mind when thinking about Bethany. She was beautiful, don't get him wrong. But how long could someone look at a pretty face?

Years ago, he didn't look twice at Brielle. He considered her like a kid sister but his feelings about her now were far from brotherly. She'd always been the smart, shy type. The kind who didn't have a big circle of friends. Her sister had referred to Brielle's personality as the best kept secret in Cattle Cove.

It took a lot to truly get to know her and he'd only seen a peek into her true wit and spark years ago. Of course, she'd been all braces and knobby knees. Even then, there was something about her eyes that had drawn him in. Not in a sexual way. That drive hadn't awakened until meeting her again as an adult with a fully formed body—and it was a damn fine one at that.

She tripped over the second to top stair, falling forward. Her hands went to the floor, his hands went to her hips to steady her and she cringed from the pain. And damned if more of that electricity sparked at his fingertips.

It was going to be a long night trying to sleep beside her. Maybe he could grab a spot on the floor? Or take the couch downstairs? It had been comfortable enough to stretch out on. Of course, coming in at six-feet four-inches, there wasn't a couch long enough to completely support him. Staying in the bedroom would be a challenge to his REM. Brielle had grown up to become temptation on a stick.

"I'm okay. Just a little clumsy. My foot went to sleep on the couch and I'm still trying to shake it off."

With his hands on those soft hips of hers, he couldn't think clearly. So, he cleared his throat and moved them to the handrails. "Okay." His voice cracked on the word. Boy, was he in trouble.

Refocusing on his own toes, he followed her up the last of the stairs.

"Is it okay if I keep the door cracked while I shower?"

He took a second to answer. "Do whatever makes you feel more comfortable. I'll be right here in the hallway."

His phone was still downstairs. There wasn't much else to distract himself with except for Bandit. "I'll just hang out with my dog."

Bandit's tail wagged even harder. There were times when Dalton believed that animal could understand words beyond basic commands.

"Thank you. For everything." She rounded on him at the top of the stairs. "In case I forget to tell you later, I appreciate all that you're doing for me."

The temptation to lean in and kiss her was a physical presence. And since he'd outgrown letting his hormones rule once he got out of high school, he practiced restraint.

"You're welcome, Brielle." Then he added, "It's actually really good to see you again. I'd forgotten how sharp your mind is and how interesting a person you are. Don't get me wrong, the circumstances are awful. Still, it's been nice to be around someone who knows me but doesn't share my last name. Is that strange?"

"I get it. I've spent so much time focusing on building my career outside of Cattle Cove that I forgot how much I loved the people here." Her cheeks flushed when she said the word, love. Like she'd caught herself saying something she shouldn't.

"It's half the reason my brothers and cousins stick around."

"And you?"

"There's no other place I'd rather be than right here." A frog had his throat on the last few words. There was a double meaning in those words that he couldn't ignore or shirk off. He was exactly where he wanted to be in the moment. And just like every other time he'd gotten close to a woman, guilt assaulted him. Would he ever be able to get over the past? Because for the first time since the car accident, he wanted to move on.

Wanting and doing were two different things. No one knew that better than him.

As if sensing the mood had shifted, Brielle turned and walked into her bedroom. He stood there, wishing words came to him to make things right. None came.

The ache in his heart had nothing to do with the past now and everything to do with the woman who walked right past him and into the bathroom.

Talk about leaving words left unsaid. Damn. Regret filled his chest the minute he heard the spigot turn on. So, basically, he was winning at the whole moving beyond his past thing. *Great, Dalton.*

Because the look in Brielle's eyes, the way they sparkled with need, pushed past a few of his carefully constructed walls. And for the first time, he wanted to break open more of that casing.

It had been so long since he'd allowed himself to truly feel anything deeper than surface attraction. An annoying voice in the back of his mind picked that moment to point out that he'd lost a mother, a future bride, and a child.

Had he connected those tragedies in his mind? Linked them when Mallory died? Decided he just had bad luck when it came to having women in his life?

Dalton sank onto the floor, a little more than shocked at the revelation. He'd dated around plenty, telling himself there was no one out there he could see himself doing long-term with. Was that true? Freud would probably have a field day with that analysis. Dalton had learned a little bit about psychology in school as a required class. But, damn. He hadn't connected any of the dots until now.

Until Brielle made him want to, the annoying little voice pointed out.

Speaking of which, the spigot turned off and she emerged from the bathroom a few minutes after. Her long hair was pulled away from her face and those freckles dotting the bridge of her nose had never been sexier than in this light.

He pushed to standing as she moved past him and straight into her bedroom. The dark towel that was cinched above full breasts contrasted against her creamy skin.

Suddenly, his tongue felt like he'd licked a glue stick. He coughed to ease the dryness in his throat. It didn't help.

The door to her bedroom was nothing more than a crack as he stood there taken back by his body's reaction to her. He shouldn't be so caught off guard except that this was Brielle Anderson, someone he'd known since she was… well…she sure didn't look this grown when he knew her before.

Dalton shoved his hands in his pants pockets to give them something to do. He almost whistled just to distract himself. Now, that was funny. He was seriously losing it. Being nervous around the opposite sex was definitely a new experience. At some point, he laughed just to break up some of the tension causing his chest to feel like truck was docked on it. His palms were sweaty. If this situation wasn't a little too real, it would actually be funny.

But, hey, Brielle was a beautiful and intelligent woman. She was warm and funny. Exactly the kind of person he could see himself spending time with under ordinary circumstances.

He walked over to her bedroom door and knocked.

"Mind if I use your shower?"

"Be my guest."

"I'll keep the door open and Bandit here can keep you company while I clean up." He figured he needed a shower and then he could make a bed downstairs.

"Okay." Her voice had a velvety quality to it that wasn't helping with the attraction thing.

He jogged downstairs and retrieved his overnight bag. Bandit had been given plenty of water and he'd been shown the bowl in case he got hungry through the night. He'd been fed and let outside to take care of business. He should be set for the rest of the evening. It was late and Dalton could feel it in his body.

Dalton took the steps two at a time until he reached the landing. Brielle stood there in an oversized T-shirt and boxers that highlighted way too much of those long, slender legs of hers. He didn't want to think about her breasts pressed against the cotton of her tee. So, yeah, that just worked out.

He thanked her as he took the towel.

"Okay if I wait right here?" she asked.

"Suit yourself."

"And, Dalton, would you mind leaving the door open so we can talk?"

He groaned before grabbing the towel and mumbling the same phrase as before.

"Sorry."

"Don't be. I just need to be a better man." He didn't add that he wanted to be a better man for her. That he wanted to push past the ghosts of the past and open his heart for her. And he sure as hell didn't detail out what he'd do to that gorgeous body of hers once she agreed to be his. "Do you have a problem with me sleeping on the couch?"

"As a matter of fact, I do."

"AND WHAT WOULD THAT BE?" Dalton's raised eyebrow was adorable. If by adorable, Brielle meant rip-your-clothes-off.

"First of all, you're here to help me, not to be uncomfortable trying to cram yourself on the couch."

"I promise you it won't be that bad and I equally promise you I've slept in far worse conditions and haven't had a problem. Anywhere inside is better than outdoors in the middle of August when there's been no rain in sight."

Well, she couldn't argue there.

So, she put her hand on her hip and tried to level him with her gaze and said, "I'm not trying to hit on you, Dalton. I really would feel horrible if I'm here enjoying my bed and you're downstairs on a cramped couch. You can't tell me that you will be able to fully stretch out on that thing. I don't care how comfortable it is. And I would put you in the guest room but—and I hate admitting this part—I'm actually pretty freaked out by what happened today not just once but twice. There were two attempts on my life in a matter of hours and now my friend is gone—"

He brought his hands up, palms out.

"Say no more. I'll do whatever you need. That's what I'm here for."

"Thank you, Dalton. I don't know how I'll ever repay you and I promise not to drag this out."

A look of disappointment darkened his features. "That's unfortunate."

"Sorry?"

"Nothing," he said.

She could stand there and try to dissect the meaning of that off-handed comment all night, or she could slide under the covers and get comfortable. Maybe even sleep. Covers won. "Meet me in my room?"

"It's a date." Dalton disappeared into the bathroom, leaving the door open. An electric toothbrush buzzed a few seconds later. Rather than stand there in the middle of the hallway and wait, Brielle made kissing noises at Bandit. He followed her as she retreated into her bedroom. She had never been happier that she'd made the investment in a king-size bed once Bandit hopped on.

Her thoughts bounced back to Sophie Freedland's husband and child. It was good that she'd left her phone and laptop downstairs, or she'd be too tempted to look up information on the company's internal communication site.

It was good to unplug, she tried to remind herself. Then again, what if the sheriff tried to reach them? Their phones would be downstairs.

Dalton took two steps into the room and then froze. "What's wrong?"

"I was just having a mental debate about not having my phone up here. I was concerned the sheriff might try to reach us, or someone else with news. What if something else happens and we can help?"

"As far as the sheriff goes, she knows where you live. If she needs one of us, she can always stop by. Believe me, she will. You've met her. She's not shy."

"No. She's not," Brielle agreed.

"Anyone else can wait until tomorrow morning. Unless you don't think you can rest without a phone up here. In which case, I can easily remedy the situation. Let me know which way you want to go on this."

"You think I should walk away from it, don't you?"

"Your opinion matters most. But, if you're asking, it seems like a good idea. We don't get near enough time away from our devices these days. Plus, the biggest threat so far has been someone coming after you. Doors are locked. I'm here."

"What about the attic? Someone was able to get inside my house while I was here. What if they come back and surprise us?"

"For one, my truck is out front. It's big and it has the McGannon Herd logo on the back window."

"People around here know you. What if the perp isn't

from around here?" She saw his reasoning and he was convincing her.

"He'll still see my truck out front. He'll assume another person is in the house with you. This guy's a coward. He won't strike if it could expose him or backfire in any way. Having two people in the house increases his risk of being identified and therefore caught. Once we know who it is, it's over for him."

"Okay." She took in a deep breath. Everything he said made perfect sense. Where was logic in a time of fear?

She exhaled a couple of times.

"But if that doesn't add up for you, then by all means I'll run downstairs—"

"No. Don't do that. You're right. That thing is glued to my hand all my waking hours." There was something freeing about stepping away for the night. It was late. The day had been traumatic. Her parents were long since asleep. They wouldn't have made it to the credits. Her sister was still early in her pregnancy. "It's a strange sensation to just decide to leave my phone downstairs but it's growing on me."

"There are plenty of spots on the ranch where I'm out of cell range. I love being disconnected from the world sometimes." He climbed in bed on top of the covers. Don't even get her started about the fact he had on a simple white T-shirt but there was nothing basic about the man's body.

Rather than sit there and drool, she asked, "Mind if I turn down the light?"

She never did like sleeping in pitch black in case she had to get up and go to the bathroom in the middle of the night. These older homes didn't have en suite. And she'd been traveling so much that half the time she forgot where she was. Having a low light gave her the ability to ground herself quickly rather than fumble around or knock the lamp off the nightstand, which she'd done more than once.

"When you first mentioned it, I'm not kidding that I almost had an anxiety attack. The idea is growing on me."

"Who needs to be reachable twenty-four hours a day, seven days a week."

"Tell my boss that." She laughed.

"Maybe you should."

"What are you saying? He'll fire me."

"Will he? Do you have to be available on a whim? Or is it just convenient for him and others at work?"

"Okay, now you're hitting a nerve because I'm thinking about times that I needed an answer from someone and didn't hear back." Did she have to be attached to her cell?

"They could be out of range or..." He wiggled his eyebrows. "Maybe they're saying no to being available on a dime."

"I always told myself being connected was the reason I got so many promotions so early in my career."

"What if it was purely the quality of your work?"

"I never tested the theory. I just got used to being the go-to person for everything." Maybe she should have at least tried. Or had work been a convenient way to shut out the world? Hide behind her busy schedule and not truly connect with anyone?

"And you still can be. Just set hours that are right for your lifestyle."

"Well, that really is funny. My lifestyle has been about work and nothing else." She could admit to feeling a certain restlessness lately. A longing that caused her to climb deeper in a cave rather than step out and face it. Because of a longing for what? A job change? A scenery change?

"I can't fault anyone else for that, considering I'm not

much better." He winked and it broke some of the tension building inside her.

Was there something wrong with her that she didn't think much about having a family? That it wasn't something she pined for or daydreamed about?

And why the longing sensation that had been plaguing her?

"You have Bandit here. That's something. I'm away so much of the time that I can't have a dog. I'd love one as sweet as this guy." Living in Cattle Cove was supposed to bring the stability she needed. So, why didn't it feel like it worked anymore?

"I'm a lucky guy."

Someone banged on the front door so hard the walls practically shook.

"Jesus, sounds like a police raid." Dalton threw off the comforter and was zipping up his jeans faster than a rattler could strike. Brielle was a little slower on the take. She grabbed the housecoat that was hanging on the back of her door.

Dalton moved with the ease and grace of a professional running back. She was nowhere near as fast. Bandit was on the move, coming in somewhere in between her and Dalton. She rounded the stairs at the same time Dalton swung the door open wide.

A surprised Kevin stood at the entry.

"What are you doing here?" Brielle asked.

Kevin's gaze flew from Dalton to her. Panic crossed his light features.

"You didn't respond to any of my texts. I got worried that maybe something had happened to you."

"Me?" She played dumb. "Why would anything happen to me?"

"I don't know." He threw his hands in the air and slurred his words. "First, the chick from legal dies at work and then you suddenly stop answering my texts."

"It's late, Kevin."

"That's never stopped you before."

12

Dalton sized up Kevin Roland.

The smell of beer on the guy's breath nearly knocked Dalton back a step. So yeah, he'd been drinking tonight. Happy hour that went on too long? He was average height with a slim build. He had brown hair and eyes—eyes that seemed to be avoiding Dalton like the plague.

"Well, I no longer answer work texts after hours."

"Since when?" Kevin drew his words out. They weren't exactly slurred but there was no way Dalton would allow the man to get behind the wheel again.

He also had to fight every instinct he had to take up Brielle's battle and tell the guy off. She was a grown woman. She was strong. She could stand up for herself.

Unless she asked him to step in on her behalf...that was a whole other ball game. He crossed his arms over his chest and stood back, enjoying the fireworks.

"I appreciate your concern, Kevin. As you can see, I'm fine. But you're not. You shouldn't be driving in your condition." She moved beside Dalton, and Kevin kept his gaze focused on her.

"Okay, well then I'll just—"

"Be on your way?" Dalton stepped forward and grabbed the man's wrist. He turned his palm facing up and took the set of keys. "Like the lady said, you shouldn't be driving under the circumstances."

The sheer look of shock on Kevin's features was priceless. He finally made eye contact with Dalton, but quickly turned away as though he'd just stared at the sun. Again, Dalton had to fight every protective instinct inside him not to say what was really on his mind as the guy swayed back and forth.

"Those are my keys," Kevin finally mustered enough courage to say.

"Look, buddy. I don't particularly care about you. If you drive away from here and meet a pole at a hundred miles an hour, that's on you. What if you tag a minivan with a family in it? And someone else dies because of your stupidity? That's on my conscience for the rest of my life because I'm the one who let you get behind the wheel after you've had too much to drink. That, I can't live with. So, the way I see it, we can do this one of two ways. You can let me drive you home, or I can call the sheriff and give you back your keys once she gets here. Make no mistake, if you get behind the wheel in front of her, you're going to jail tonight." Dalton could almost hear the wheels grinding in the guy's head. "Your choice. What's it gonna be?"

Kevin took a step back and had to grab onto the doorjamb to keep his balance. The man seemed to know better than to argue. "I'll take you up on your offer for a ride home."

This would give Dalton the added benefit of finding out

where the guy lived. Kevin also just jumped up on Dalton's suspect list. Showing up unannounced and after drinking under the guise of caring was at the very least passive-aggressive behavior.

Coward? Sizing Kevin up one more time, Dalton could tick that box. He turned to Brielle and lowered his voice. "I can drive this guy if you want to follow in my truck."

"I should get dressed if we're heading out."

"We'll wait right here for you."

Brielle's gaze bounced from Dalton to Kevin and back. Concern caused worry lines to score her forehead.

Dalton smiled when he realized what she was worried about. "He'll still be in one piece when you get back."

"I'll hurry."

As promised, she darted up the stairs. If her hip was still hurting, she ignored the pain or at the very least was able to push through it.

Dalton wasn't worried about Kevin. The longer he stood there, the more he swayed back and forth. And then his gaze darted to the right, toward freedom. Drunk people were funny. They gave everything away.

"Don't do it, Kevin."

"Excuse me?"

"Here's the deal. I just promised to deliver you to your house in one piece and I can't do that if you take off running, so—"

"Hold on. Hold on. What makes you think I'll run?"

"Call me a mind reader."

Kevin looked very confused and a little like he'd been busted sticking his hand in the cookie jar before dinner.

"Do us both a favor and stand right where you are until Brielle gets back, so I don't have to explain to her why you're on the ground and I'm sitting on top of you because you can't outrun me."

Kevin nodded. His eyes squinted, practically closed. He seemed to get the message.

The sounds of footsteps on the staircase said Brielle was coming. She really did change in record time. Bandit was by her side and Dalton didn't want to acknowledge how right it felt to see the two of them together.

"Ready?" The sound of her voice was a rain shower in the middle of a drought.

"See. Told you I wouldn't do anything to him," Dalton whispered as she turned up next to him.

"Thank you."

"You can thank me later." He probably shouldn't have said that. But, damn, with her fresh-picked flower scent flooding his senses every time he breathed, he was bound to slip up every once in a while.

Her smile reddened her cheeks and his heart took another hit.

"Maybe I will." With that, she moved into the kitchen and retrieved her handbag. She picked up his keys on the coffee table where he'd left them next to his phone a few hours ago. And she brought his phone over.

"Thank you," he said as he took the cell. Their fingers grazed and a jolt of electricity woke him up. No need for caffeine after that, except that he planned to stop for some at the nearest convenience store anyway. When it came to his caffeine, he didn't play.

Dalton turned his attention back to Kevin, who seemed to be standing on two blades of grass in a breeze. "What's your address, Kevin?"

He rattled off an address that, when Dalton looked it up

on his phone, was a solid forty-five-minute drive from there. He was definitely going to need that coffee.

So Kevin was clear and for other reasons Dalton didn't want to overthink, he leaned in and kissed Brielle on the lips. He told himself he was doing it to get the guy to back off, but that wasn't exactly the whole truth.

BRIELLE CAUGHT Dalton's gaze after the kiss. He most likely did it as a favor to show Kevin that she was already in a relationship, but the look in Dalton's eyes said there was more to the story. She *wanted* there to be more. Because her feelings were out of control at this point and a piece of her wished he was in the same boat.

Don't get her wrong, he'd been clear there was an attraction between them. No one could fake the chemistry in the kisses they'd shared or the fact their emotions could go from zero to full throttle in a matter of seconds when they gave in to the storm brewing between them. But where would it go? He had the ranch. She had her job. The only thing connecting them was their shared connection to a town they both loved. The restless feeling in her chest was growing, though, and she was starting to think it might be best to move. Austin?

"Can Bandit ride with me?" She didn't want to leave him home alone and she could use the company on the ride over.

"He'd like that." Dalton turned to Kevin. "Lead me to your vehicle."

Kevin drove a sports car. Dalton took one look at the red vehicle that was low to the ground and said, "This will be interesting."

"Come on, Bandit." Brielle walked to the pickup, waited patiently for her to open the door, and then hopped inside. He made himself comfortable in the middle of the bench seat and she pulled herself up and into the driver's seat. Her hip reminded her that it wasn't too happy. The few hours of rest she'd gotten this evening helped. She'd always been a fast healer. Her parents had joked that healing was her superpower when she was a kid.

Brielle watched as Dalton wedged himself inside the low-profile vehicle. It would be funny if this whole situation with Kevin wasn't strange. He gave her the creeps. Having Dalton around sure stopped Kevin cold. Good. He had no business showing up to her place. He could blame it on alcohol all he wanted but his behavior was most certainly not okay.

She would talk to HR about him when she returned to work next week. With everything going on, she decided it might be best to take a couple days of vacation. She had enough stacking up. She might as well take a few.

Navigating down her street, she realized just what a sleepy town she lived in. Cattle Cove suited her. The shine had worn off being on the road for work long ago. And yet, she'd gotten comfortable there. She'd gotten into a routine. And even though it didn't suit her or her lifestyle anymore, she'd stuck with it out of habit.

Time to make some changes. It was strange how it sometimes took a big event to shake things up. Like she needed to be shaken down to the core to reset her priorities. Or maybe just realize what they were. The events of the past twenty-or so hours were stripping down all the nonsense in her life. She was beginning to see with such clarity now. Her job was no longer a good fit. Didn't mean she planned to run in tomorrow and turn in her notice. The time had come for a new beginning. Maybe she could take a couple of weeks off to figure out what she really wanted to do next.

The heavy weight that sat docked on her chest was starting to break up. A lightheartedness that she hadn't felt in more years than she cared to count was settling in its place.

Bandit was asleep and snoring by the time they hit the highway. There were a few vehicles on the road. Almost half an hour later, they took the off ramp. On the service road, they came up to a red light.

Dalton made a left turn, hitting the light just before it changed. She got stuck. A vehicle came roaring up from behind and before she could react, it wheeled in front of her and cut her off, blocking her from making the turn. The first word that came to mind was, *jerk*. And then she realized the windows of the SUV were blacked out.

Panic roared through her as her pulse skyrocketed. She reached for the gear shift and slammed it in reverse. She mashed the gas pedal and her head flew forward as the truck sped backward.

She checked all around her and got her first break when there were no cars behind her. Jamming her foot on the brake, she put her right hand on Bandit to keep him from being thrown onto the floorboard. He was awake and popped up to standing.

"It's okay, Bandit. Hang on for me, buddy." She turned the wheel to the left and hit the gas pedal, swerving at the last minute to avoid the SUV. She took a hard left and found herself going in the opposite direction of Dalton. A quick glance in the rearview told her the SUV followed her. There was another set of headlights that were low to the ground. They had to belong to the sports car Dalton was driving. In fact, the low headlights zipped around the side of the SUV so fast they were practically a blur.

The road narrowed to a two-lane highway as Brielle barreled down it, spitting gravel from beneath her tires. The sports car fell in rank, between her and the SUV. The vehicle Dalton drove was too small. It would be no match for the SUV.

From the mirror, she saw the SUV getting dangerously close to Dalton. She immediately shot into the oncoming traffic lane to let him pass her. His truck would be a better match against the SUV.

Dalton refused to take the opening. Instead, he flashed his lights at her, telling her to get back over. The SUV swerved into the lane, closing the gap between the two of them and edging the sports car out. Dalton zipped in between them in just enough time to stop the SUV.

Brielle gunned the engine, straddling both lanes by driving in the center of the road. The move should cut down on the back and forth between lanes. She was driving fast. Too fast. One slip up and the guy in the SUV wouldn't have to kill her.

She also had Bandit to think about. He'd been tossed onto the floorboard where he stayed. So, she slowed down, forcing the procession to reduce their speed. She had no idea if the SUV driver had a weapon. Part of her thought they would have used it by now. Right?

It was a gamble but what other choice did she have? Outrun him? Try to drive until his gas tank was on E?

She didn't know the area and it was remote enough not to have police stations nearby. There'd be a sheriff's office. Maybe Dalton could call Sheriff Justice and arrange for local law enforcement to meet up with them.

Where was her phone? She risked a glance on the floorboard where she'd set it down. The handbag was nowhere in sight, but its contents had spilled out everywhere. She heard a crunch, the sound of bumper crashing into bumper.

Okay, okay.

She sped up to give Dalton some breathing room from the SUV. The truck had a good engine. It was solid, but not exactly what she would call nimble.

Her phone was somewhere out of reach and she was racing down a two-lane road late at night. No streetlights. Just curves and bounces until she thought her brains might fall out.

At this hour, no one else was on the street, if she could call it that. She had no idea where she was. Oh, right. Didn't all vehicles have an emergency function now?

Dalton had to have already thought of calling the law. And he had Kevin in the vehicle. He might be drunk but an event like this might sober him up. Either way, he was lucid enough to find her house. He would be able to call 911.

A buzzing noise filled the cab as she bounced around. Her cell. Dalton?

She felt around under the driver's seat. Nothing. If only Bandit could help.

Dalton flashed his lights and she had no idea what he was trying to say. She risked a glance at the map on the dashboard. Water. A lake. Straight ahead. No streetlights and a winding road while traveling at a high rate of speed.

So, no, this situation couldn't get much worse.

13

"Tell her your address and then tell her where you think we are." Dalton handed over the phone to Kevin. He'd told Sheriff Justice their approximate location and, since they were out of her jurisdiction, she was patching through to local law enforcement.

There was a lake ahead and the roads were about to get real. He could handle the twists and turns in the sports car, but the truck would never make it. Brielle would bust through a guard rail, if there was one, and end up in the lake with Bandit. He couldn't lose her or his furry buddy.

She was speeding to give him a break, but she had to slow down. She was running out of time.

His pulse was jacked through the roof. Kevin here was no help. He'd started crying—crying!—the minute Dalton banked a U-turn after he saw what the SUV had done to Brielle. Granted, Dalton had to drive on the wrong side of the road to get back to the intersection and zip through a red light to position the sports car in between her and the SUV, but still. Yes, the move had been risky. The bet had paid off.

Dalton was about eighty percent certain Kevin took a

leak on himself. He was drunk, so being in a high-speed car chase without knowing what was going on probably made it a reasonable reaction. One that Dalton would rather not smell. He was going to have a lot to say about Brielle's coworker once they were in the clear.

There hadn't been much he could do in this matchbox size vehicle against an SUV and a dual cab pickup truck except act as a buffer. Dear old Kevin had most likely peed on himself a second time when the SUV slammed into the bumper. He'd cried something about the car being new and in perfect condition. And then he'd mumbled something about being too young to die. Not exactly the guy Dalton would pick to play on a sports team. Or the kind of guy who would have someone else's back in an emergency.

But after tonight, he had a feeling neither he nor Brielle would be seeing much of Kevin.

The thought shouldn't make him want to smile. What could he say? He was no saint and Kevin was a turd. He was also not guilty.

"She wants to talk to you." Kevin held the phone out.

"Put the call on speaker and hold the phone out toward me." He didn't want to touch anything after Kevin had his hands on it. Not without sanitizing it first. But the main reason was he needed to keep both hands on the steering wheel. The fancy car wasn't meant for the kind of beating it was taking. He would cover whatever insurance premium needed to be paid. Hell, he'd pay to replace the vehicle at no cost to Kevin. The guy didn't ask for any of this. Maybe it would teach him a lesson about sticking his nose where it doesn't belong or showing up at someone's house unwanted.

"I'm here," he said into the phone.

"The nearest deputy is half an hour away from you. The only good news is you're driving toward him." Sheriff Justice sounded wide awake and he wondered when she ever slept. Job hazard?

"There's trouble on the road ahead. If I can't get Brielle to slow down, she'll end up in that trouble."

"I can get an ambulance headed your way if you think it's a good idea," she said.

"I'll take all the help I can get." The car bounced, knocking the phone out of Kevin's hand.

"Sorry." He scrambled around to find it, leaned forward, and when the car bounced again, he cracked his head on the dashboard. The smell of alcohol and urine wasn't helping matters.

When he reclaimed the phone and brought it back within reasonable distance to Dalton's mouth, he said, "You can take Kevin's name off the suspect list."

"Suspect?" The shock in that one word seemed sobering. Kevin sat up a little straighter. He tried to focus his eyes.

"Okay." She drew the word out like she expected an explanation later.

There was no way Kevin was an accomplice to the guy behind the wheel of the SUV. He would have cracked by now and spilled his guts. What Dalton couldn't figure was how the SUV driver found them. He must have been watching Brielle's house.

"What can you tell me about the vehicle and driver that I don't already know?"

"I can confirm the suspect is male. Can't get a good enough look to give hair color." The view in his rearview gave him nothing to work with. Blacked out windows made a side view impossible. The windshield might not be blacked out, but the driver was basically a ghost. His sunglasses reflected light and they were the only things visible in the otherwise dark cab.

The lake was getting closer and the roads were about to get real. If Brielle didn't hit the brakes soon, it would be too late. This was the worst game of chicken Dalton had ever played.

Just when he thought it was hopeless, the SUV slowed down. Dalton flashed his headlights and relief washed over him the minute Brielle hit the brakes. He white-knuckled the steering wheel, praying it wasn't too late.

The SUV stopped, turned, and sped off in the opposite direction.

The truck in front of him slowed to a reasonable speed. Dalton could feel his heartbeat in his throat.

"My God." It was all Kevin said. All he had to say.

"We're okay," Dalton shouted to the phone. He stopped the sports car and turned to Kevin. "If you see headlights behind us, don't wait for me. Get in the driver's seat and get out of here. He isn't after you."

The dashboard lit Kevin's face. It was basically the color of a bleached-white sheet. Kevin nodded.

Dalton bolted out of the driver's side and toward two of the most important things in his life—Brielle and Bandit.

"Are you hurt?" The words flew out of his mouth as the driver's side door opened.

"I'm okay. Bandit is fine. We're both shaken up. That's all." Her hands shook as she cleared the driver's seat and then threw her arms around his neck. Bandit exited the vehicle on her heels.

He hauled Brielle against his chest as he visually scanned Bandit, who walked fine as he trotted over to the grass, and then relieved himself. So, yeah, he was doing all right.

"I don't know what I would have done if I'd lost you," he whispered in her ear. A very large part of him didn't want to ever be that exposed again. Pain the level of a tsunami threatened to drag him under, and then rip him to shreds before tossing him out to sea where he'd be lost.

What he needed most was to erect more walls. He would if he could. They might come later. Right now, all he wanted to do was breathe in her scent another second before they had to split apart so he could get them to safety.

A door slammed behind him and tires screeched. Dalton spun around to watch the sports car barrel down the road in the opposite direction. There were no other headlights in view as Dalton scanned the area.

"Oh, no. Is he okay to drive?" Brielle asked, panic laced her tone.

"I think the last half hour sobered him up." Dalton laughed. "I know I shouldn't find it funny… But it kind of is."

"Remind me to ask you about that later."

Dalton moved behind Brielle and wrapped his arms around her. She leaned against his chest, her warmth refilling a well that had been dry far too long.

Bandit trotted over and stopped next to the driver's side door.

"Good idea, Bandit." Dalton leaned in and brushed a kiss on Brielle's neck. "Are you ready to get out of here?"

"Take me home."

"I have a better idea," he said. "I'd rather take you to the ranch. How does that sound?"

She seemed to think about it for a long moment.

"I like that idea a lot actually."

"Good. His heart gave a traitorous flip at the thought of Brielle being in his home. "I better update the sheriff. She has a deputy on the way and an ambulance."

Dalton was halfway toward reaching for his pocket when he realized Kevin just pulled away with his cell.

"Your coworker just drove off with my phone."

Brielle was starting to realize there would be a story about Kevin once she and Dalton were settled. "To think I was jealous you had someone else in the car with you who could actually use a cell phone."

"Yeah. Kevin wasn't much help. And I doubt he'll be talking to you much anymore, let alone bothering you in any way." The corners of Dalton's mouth upturned despite him trying to hold a serious expression. Jealous?

"Well, that's a relief. Showing up at my house unannounced was definitely a shock and wholly inappropriate for a working relationship. I'd planned to report him to HR once I go back to the office."

Dalton took her by the hand. She couldn't help but notice how small hers was by comparison. His fingers were calloused, rough against her skin. She liked the feel of her hand in his. He walked her to the passenger side and helped her locate her scattered belongings.

"This whole ordeal has me rethinking a few things in my life," she admitted. "I haven't taken a vacation this year. It might be time to take a few days off and reprioritize."

The muscles in Dalton's hand stiffened.

"Yeah? What did you have in mind?" he asked, and his voice matched his body language.

Did he think she was asking him for some sort of commitment?

"Never mind, Dalton. I can see that I'm talking to the wrong person about my personal life." The words came out sharper than she'd intended. What could she say? She was hurt and having a difficult time covering it up.

"Hold on. I wasn't trying to say that—"

"No. You weren't. I didn't say you were." Now, it was her body's turn to tense up. She felt around beneath the passenger seat. Her hand met a familiar object, her phone. "Found it."

She held up her cell.

"Go ahead and make whatever call you need to." She folded her arms, daring him to say another word to her.

He put his hands up, palms out. "Can we talk later?"

Well, she didn't expect them to have a conversation out here.

"Yes."

"Good. Because I need to reach the sheriff and I—"

"Dalton. We've known each other for a long time. You don't have to play nice with me. I get it. We're friends. I was talking to you *as* a friend. There's nothing else to discuss." She walked away toward the back of the pickup, got halfway there when she realized she wasn't the one driving now.

Circling back, she met Dalton's chest.

"For what it's worth, I'm sorry."

She threw a shoulder into his arm as she walked past. *I'm sorry* were her least favorite words. She mumbled them anyway.

Dalton made the call as she sat in the passenger seat, fighting the hot tears threatening. It was more than just their conversation that threatened to bring on the onslaught. All the events stacked on top of the conversation were chipping away at her resolve. A few of those tears rolled down her cheeks. She was able to dry them up by the time Dalton claimed the driver's seat.

After a quick update, the drive to the ranch was spent in silence. Dalton pulled up in front of his cabin-style house, and then parked. The place was palatial by comparison to her two-bedroom home in town.

At this point, it was straight up the middle of the night. Adrenaline had faded and exhaustion seeped into Brielle's bones.

"The sheriff said she'd swing by in a few hours to take your statement," Dalton said as he cut off the engine.

Brielle nodded. There was an oversized parking garage that looked big enough to fit three cars and she noted he'd opted to park out front. He also dropped the keys in the floorboard rather than take them with him. Ranch life at its finest.

She exited the vehicle and walked toward the front door, thinking how much was changing in Cattle Cove. The town could no longer deem itself safe for families if the crime rate continued to climb. Sheriff Justice must be frustrated. She seemed the type to take her role seriously.

Dalton held out his hand and she realized her cell was on his palm. She thanked him as she took it.

"Hey," he started as they approached the front door.

"Does what you're about to say relate to the case or my safety for the next few hours?" She wasn't trying to be a jerk, even though she could admit to sounding like one. What could she say? She was hurt from his action earlier. She was human.

"No. It doesn't." There was a hint of defeat in his voice that almost had her wishing she'd taken a different tact.

"Then, can we table it for now? I could barely keep my eyes open the last twenty minutes of the drive here and I have a feeling tomorrow is going to be another long day. I want nothing more than to lay my head down and rest."

Dalton nodded. A look passed behind his eyes that she couldn't quite pinpoint but made her heart sink in her chest anyway. Hurt? Disappointment? Frustration? Maybe a little bit of all three?

He opened the door—opened, not unlocked, she noted —and held the door for her.

This was the first time inside his place, and she was too tired to notice much besides the low-lighting, open-concept, and calming interior. His home had a masculine quality that was equally upscale. The type of sophisticated that looked effortless.

"The master is this way." He started toward a hallway to the left of the living/dining/kitchen area.

"And the guest room?"

"I'll take the guest room tonight."

"I'm not kicking you out of your bed, Dalton."

He stood there, studying her for a long moment. Rather than put up an argument, he said, "Right this way."

She followed him down the opposite hallway to a guest room that was bigger than her master back home. She loved her house, don't get her wrong, but there was something about new construction that fit all the pieces together of the way people lived now. That, and new plumbing. Her house had all the history and charm she could want but pipes that could barely hold a flush.

Instead of looking brand new and cookie-cutter, Dalton's house fit him to a T. There was nothing pretentious about it. There was a warmth to it that made her feel right at home. It wasn't stuffy. The colors were warm neutrals. The four-poster bed in the guest room looked hand-carved, and prob-ably was. There was a dresser that was truly more of a wardrobe. "Bath is over here. You should find everything you need in there if you want to wash up before bed."

"Where does that door lead?"

"En suite bathroom."

She didn't mean to blink at him. He had a guest suite? She'd been to the ranch with her sister years ago, but they'd always stayed in the big house. This one wasn't even a spark in Dalton's imagination yet.

The care and attention to detail was evident everywhere she looked. It was probably the day's events and the fact that they'd just been chased by the SUV, but the thought of him sleeping way on the opposite side of the house didn't sit well. She needed a couple of days to get her bearings again before she could comfortably be alone again.

"What is it?" Dalton picked up on her mood change.

Should she lie? Tell him it was nothing?

Brielle issued a sharp sigh.

"This room is beautiful—"

"But?" His forehead creased with concern and her heart thought it might crack.

She shifted her weight from her left foot to her right and twisted her fingers together.

"Go ahead. You can tell me anything, Brielle. I'm not here to judge or make your life any harder. In fact, it's quite the opposite."

"It just doesn't sound like me in my head to admit that I'm still scared. I thought I could do it. I should be able to sleep in this room alone." There. She'd said it.

14

"Being scared doesn't make you weak." Dalton repeated the words a couple of times in his own head. He needed the reminder as much as anyone. His fear didn't have anything to do with her stalker. At least, he wasn't afraid for himself. But he could have lost her tonight. And that scared the hell out of him.

She exhaled slowly.

"I've always prided myself on my independence."

"Nothing's changed." One look into her eyes and he could see that he wasn't being very convincing. "I won't go down the road of telling you how much you've been through or that most people wouldn't still be standing if they were in your position." He put his hand in the air to stop her from putting up an argument. "Here's the thing. When a job is too big or too dangerous for one person on the ranch, we call in back up. It could be tracking poachers or pulling a cow out of the mud. Does that make us less in any way in your eyes?"

"No. That's just being smart."

"Exactly." He studied her, hoping his logic was getting through because she was one of the strongest people he'd ever met. That was the thing about strong people. It took a lot for them to break and they usually had a stubborn streak a mile long that made them travel too long on the road before raising a flag. That same streak was their downfall. They were too stubborn to give up or give in, until the dam broke.

"Then, maybe you won't take this the wrong way when I ask you to let me sleep in your bed."

"I didn't think you wanted to take the master."

"With you."

"Done. Do you want to stay in here and get ready for bed? There's a robe in the bathroom you can change into and there should be a couple pairs of pajamas."

She shot him a look.

"Before you go getting any ideas, Miss Penny keeps this place stocked. Not me. That goes with the food in the fridge too. Before you open it and think I'm some kind of gourmet cook, you should know I'm not the one who stocked the kitchen."

"I know how hard you guys work. It's really nice of her to still take care of you."

"We've tried to get her to stop, but she refuses. Says it's no trouble and that she enjoys it. To tell the truth, her cooking feels like home. I'm not one to argue about food being replenished before I open my mouth to express a need. I count myself as lucky and move on."

"I don't blame you one bit."

"Do you think accepting her help makes me weak in any way?"

She stared at him long and hard, arms folded across her chest. "Point taken."

"Good." He sat down on the edge of the bed. "I'll wait for you to get ready."

Dalton forced his gaze away from her sweet bottom as she moved into the next room. She kept the door open and he heard an electric toothbrush turn on followed by the spigot. She cracked the door and he assumed she was changing out of her clothes.

When she returned a few minutes later, she looked ready for bed.

"Follow me." He pushed to standing and started the trek into the other room when he felt a hand on his forearm.

"Thank you for reminding me that I'm doing okay under the circumstances."

He didn't turn or flinch. He didn't want to give away the effect her touch was having on him. Eyes forward, he said, "You're welcome. And you'd do the same for me."

She would. That had always been her nature even when she was younger. She'd always been the person who would push her own feelings aside, step in, and make someone else feel better. She and her sister were opposites in pretty much every way.

Looking back, there wasn't much more to his relationship with the older sister than a crush. Once he'd gotten to know Bethany, the attraction had fizzled out. Even then, he'd wanted more from a relationship than a beautiful shell. Don't get him wrong, Bethany was popular. She was nice, got good grades in school. Guys lined up for a chance to ask her out.

All physical.

But, hey, there wasn't a whole lot of substance to be found in teenagers. The nature of self-obsession made it difficult to get past the surface with anyone.

His relationship with Mallory went beyond the surface and look where that had gotten him. To be fair, if the two of them met today, he seriously doubted they would have lasted as long. That was the thing about getting older. He realized a lot faster who he wanted to spend his time with and who he didn't. He could see through their bull quicker than a bronco could buck his rider.

He could also tell the real deal when he met her. Brielle was special.

Dalton walked straight to the bedroom. "Go ahead and take the bed. I can sleep on a chair at this point. All I need is twenty minutes anyway."

"That's silly. Come to bed. We've technically already slept together twice anyway." She smiled through a yawn.

"I'll be right there." He nodded toward the bed and then moved into the en suite. He left the door open while he washed his face and brushed his teeth.

By the time he returned, she was under the covers. Bandit was already asleep. He slid in on the opposite side, and then she scooted over and curled up in the crook of his arm. Her flowery scent filled his senses and he prayed he'd be able to relax enough to grab a few minutes of sleep.

Dalton thought about the fact they could cross Kevin off the list of suspects. Which left four people he'd like to see interviewed by Sheriff Justice. She would never agree to let him watch.

The actions taken by the perp in the past twenty-four hours screamed of desperation. Someone was desperate to get Brielle out of the picture. Or make sure no one else could have her. The actions might be desperate, but they were also aggressive. This guy was a coward who hid inside a vehicle.

Dalton closed his eyes and, much to his surprise, nodded off.

He woke with a start. A quick glance at the alarm on the nightstand said he'd been asleep two hours.

And then he heard someone knocking on the door. His pulse rate jacked up as he peeled a deeply asleep Brielle's arm off him. He slipped out of the covers and tried to locate his jeans in the dark. He found them where he'd left them and managed to slip into them without falling over. He raced to the front door, hoping to catch whoever was knocking before they gave up and took off.

He opened the door to see his brother Jack standing there.

"What's going on?" he asked.

"Dad called a breakfast meeting in an hour and no one has been able to get ahold of you to let you know. I volunteered to stop by since you're on my way in." Jack blinked a couple of times. "Is everything all right here?"

"Oh, yeah. Sorry about that. Something happened to my phone. Long story, but it's gone and not coming back. But thanks for coming out here." He could track Kevin down to retrieve it, but it might be better to get a new one. His was old anyway. He would need to call and have the service shut off on that phone.

"No problem. It was on my way." Jack shrugged. "Are you good?"

"I'm helping out a friend. She's had a rough time lately. I've been distracted and it's part of the reason my phone is now gone."

"You can pick up a new one from Miss Penny in the office. Can you come up to the big house for the meeting or should I ask Dad to reschedule?"

"I'll be there. How long did you say I have?"

"An hour, give or take."

Dalton nodded. "I should be good."

"Let me know if you need anything in the meantime," Jack said.

"Do you mind letting everyone know that the sheriff will be swinging by to get a statement from Brielle soon? I'll tell Laney to swing by the big house instead of here."

"Gotcha." Jack turned toward his ride.

"Hey, bro. I know I don't say this nearly enough, but thanks for always having my back."

"Goes both ways." Jack came back and brought Dalton into a bear hug. "Whatever's going on, you know I feel the same way. And I said it before but I'm here whenever you need me. No explanation needed."

"Thank you." Dalton couldn't help but wonder about Brielle's support system. But then, most families weren't as close as the McGannons. An undeniable piece of him wanted to be hers.

BRIELLE FELT AROUND on the bed, panicked when she couldn't feel Dalton. She sat up and threw off the covers. It was dark in his room, so she flipped on the light.

He was gone.

Noises came from down the hallway. Voices?

Instead of waiting for Dalton, she climbed out of bed and moved down the hallway to check on him. He was there with his brother Jack.

"Sorry. Didn't mean to interrupt."

"I didn't realize you were awake," Dalton said.

"I wasn't until a minute ago."

Jack's gaze shifted from her to Dalton and back. To his credit, he didn't say anything about the fact she'd come from the master bedroom hallway, which he had to have noticed. Nothing was going on between her and Dalton. At least, nothing officially.

"Good to see you, Brielle," Jack said, and she exhaled a little bit. She was unsure of the reception she'd get from his family but should have known a McGannon would be nothing but welcoming.

"You too, Jack." She managed a smile that he returned.

Dalton reached for her hand and linked their fingers like it was the most normal and casual thing.

If Jack noticed, he didn't give his reaction away. Instead, he smiled and said, "See you at the house in a little while."

"We'll be there."

Jack disappeared off the porch as Dalton closed the door.

"What's that about?" she asked.

"Family meeting. Mind if we talk to the sheriff at the big house?"

"Kill two birds with one stone?" She instantly regretted her choice of words. "Forget I said that."

"How about coffee?"

"Sounds like heaven."

Dalton led her into the kitchen, their hands still linked. "My dad called a family meeting. I'm guessing he wants to explain why we have a brother we never knew about who happens to be six months older than Levi."

"Oh, no. Levi loves being the oldest in the family. Even I knew that years ago and he was way above my grade in school." She opened a couple of cabinets, looking for coffee mugs as he manned the machine.

"I don't think Kurt, that's his name, is planning to step in and take over for Levi, but it has been an interesting dynamic adding him, his new wife, and his daughter into the fold."

"Didn't your parents have a really strong marriage before your mother's accident?"

"I always believed so. As did my brothers."

"I'm sure there's a reason. I've never heard anything bad about your parents, Dalton."

"Secrets. I hate 'em. I know firsthand how they eat away at people. And yet, my dad never once gave me the impression he had a kid out there. According to Kurt, he and his mother never received any child support or care."

"Well, that really doesn't sound like your dad."

"Not to me, either. And, yet, the DNA matches." He sounded frustrated and understandably so.

"And yet, the family has accepted Kurt?"

"Well, none of this is his fault and he's our blood. What else would we do?"

"Not everyone would be so nice to him." Would her sister be so supportive? It had only been the two of them and they'd come from a loving home. Their dad had always been the rock of the family while their mother had always been...fragile. Brielle couldn't imagine being so dependent on everyone around her for the most basic of life necessities. For instance, her mother never learned to drive. How?

Brielle and her sister both got their licenses the minute they could. Brielle often wondered how happy her mother could be. She didn't have a lot of friends. Her entire world revolved around Brielle's father, who was great, don't get her wrong.

"You don't think your family would?"

"Are you kidding me right now? I think news like that would break my mother. She's so dependent on Dad. I often wonder what will happen to her if he goes first. You know? Will she wither away?" She handed over the mugs. "I mean, seriously. I love my parents, but she can't do anything without Dad. I never thought it was healthy. You know?"

"Now that I think about it, I don't believe I've ever seen your mom without your dad."

"Because she doesn't drive. She has no hobbies. No outside friendships. It just doesn't seem normal to me. But then, I look at my sister and I think she's going down the same path. Ever since she got married, it's Tim this and Tim wants that. I feel like she has no identity anymore. That's weird, right?"

He poured coffee in her cup.

"I mean, if I ever settle down...and that's a big *if*...I'd need to still be my own person," she added for no good reason except she wanted to hear herself say it. Her greatest fear in life was becoming like her mother.

Wow. There. She acknowledged the thought. She was terrified of becoming her mother and losing her identity in a relationship. Her dad wasn't a bad guy, either. Her mother had willingly given herself up as a person. Brielle couldn't think of a much worse fate.

15

"I might be the worst person ever."

"You couldn't be." Dalton shook his head as he took a sip of coffee.

"I just realized that I've stayed away from serious relationships because I'm afraid that I'll turn into my mother."

"That doesn't make you a bad person. A lot of people don't want to turn into one of their parents or both."

"I guess."

Based on her reaction, he wasn't getting through to her. Talk was cheap and overrated. So, he walked over and kissed her.

"I know that I don't want to repeat my father's mistakes. My mom is more memory than anything else at this point. I was too young to really get to know her. My memories with her are happy, though. And I can't help but think she didn't deserve to be cheated on. I can only imagine how embarrassing that might have been for her. Here's the thing. I don't know the whole story. I don't know why she forgave my father. I have to trust that was the right decision for her even if it wasn't the path I would have chosen."

"True." She took a sip of coffee and he could tell she understood his logic. "I guess I'm just never going to lose myself in a relationship in the same way as my mother."

"There's nothing wrong with that. And, whoever is lucky enough to be in a relationship with you shouldn't expect you to."

His comment netted a smile. He couldn't resist leaning in for another kiss. "Have I told you how beautiful you are first thing in the morning?"

"Is it morning?" She practically beamed. "And, no, you haven't."

"Then I've sorely neglected my job."

She pressed up to her tiptoes and planted a kiss on his lips. She tasted like dark roast coffee, his favorite.

"You're beautiful," he said again.

"You're not so bad yourself," she said with a smile. "But, please tell me if I ever turn into my mother."

"Deal." He had no idea how long he would have Brielle in his life, but he already wanted more. "We should probably get ready."

Bandit had sauntered out, so Dalton fed his buddy and then let him outside to do his business. He locked the door when Bandit returned. It was odd to lock his door out here on the property, but he figured it would give Brielle peace of mind. Plus, he didn't want to risk anyone being able to breach security. There was too much at stake.

Fifteen minutes later, they were dressed and headed toward the big house. Twenty minutes after that, they were parked and walking in the back door via the porch.

The mood in the kitchen was upbeat. Dalton instinctively reached for Brielle's hand, linking their fingers. He didn't want her to feel uncomfortable. At least, that's what he told himself anyway.

"Good morning," Miss Penny approached them first. She pulled a cell phone out of her apron. "Jack called ahead after leaving your house and said you might need this."

"Thank you." He didn't have a SIM card, so he'd have to start over.

"I preloaded everyone's name in your contacts along with Hawk and the guys. Don't worry about canceling your old phone. It's already been done." Hawk was the ranch foreman. Speculation was running wild that he and Miss Penny were an item. If so, they weren't ready to go public with their relationship. Even so, she blushed when she mentioned him by name, and he couldn't count the number of times in recent weeks he'd walked into a room only to find them paired up in quiet conversation. Miss Penny had never laughed so much or been so secretive. She had also never looked so happy and he hated that she tucked her emotions away whenever he walked into the room. If she and Hawk were an item, Dalton had nothing but good thoughts for them.

"I appreciate it." He took the cell from her and tucked it into his pocket. Then, he gave her a hug. "We would walk into walls around here if it wasn't for you."

That elicited an ear-to-ear smile. He hoped she knew how sincere he was being. She'd sacrificed her own life to be there for him, his brothers, and cousins. She needed to know how much she meant to him.

"You guys would be fine."

"Only because you brought us up to be." He gave credit where credit was due. If they were good men, she deserved the credit.

Miss Penny's eyes shifted to Brielle. "It's been a long time."

"So good to see you again, Miss Penny." Brielle beamed at her, and a thousand campfires lit inside Dalton.

Reed walked past, mumbled a greeting, and kept going until he claimed a seat at the table in between his brothers Hayden and Coby.

Dalton would swear the temperature dropped twenty degrees in the room.

Miss Penny frowned.

"He needs time to work through it," Dalton said quietly. At least, he hoped the statement was true. His brothers and cousins had always been close and the chasm growing in the family was throwing off the ease of their relationships. For their sake, Dalton prayed his uncle had nothing to do with the accident.

"I hope so. I hate seeing what this is doing to your relationships." She made a tsk sound.

"They'll heal. We might have to work at it, but we'll get there." He couldn't imagine a world in which they weren't able to work through any challenge together. "We just need to be patient and give them the space they need. I can't pretend to understand what it must be like in their position right now."

Miss Penny gave a reluctant nod.

"Thank you all for coming." Dad stood up and the room quieted. He looked each nephew in the eyes before continuing, "I'm genuinely sorry for the situation we find ourselves in and I wish more than anything that I could clear this up." He threw his hands in the air. "The truth is that I can't remember what happened." He knocked on his head. "The blow to my noggin seems to have hit an erase button. The sheriff is on her way over so we can retrace my steps. She thinks it might jog a memory and I'm willing to do anything to figure out the truth if it can get my brother out of jail."

Dalton wished he shared his father's confidence in Uncle Donny's innocence.

"That's not the reason I asked you all to be here." Dad looked each of his sons in the eyes, stopping last on Kurt's. "In some ways, what happens next is between me and Kurt. In fact, he asked me if I'd rather have this conversation in private first. When I did a little digging, he thought he might save me some embarrassment that way. As much as I appreciate his concern for me, I realize my actions affect the family. Not just mine." He scanned the room. "But all of our actions affect each other's lives. The old pebble in the pond, the ripples, couldn't be truer than they are today."

A few heads nodded.

Dalton leaned against the granite island, tugging at Brielle's hand to follow suit. She did, tucking herself behind his arm as best she could.

"I owe all of you an apology." Dad hung his shoulders in shame.

Miss Penny's toe started tapping out a rhythm against the tile flooring.

"I could come up with an excuse for having a child outside of my marriage, but I won't. This is my responsibility. My choice. And it's important for you all to know that your mother did nothing wrong."

The taps moved to double time.

"I violated your mother's trust." His eyes were cast down and regret shrouded him like a heavy blanket. "Trust that I didn't deserve in the first place."

Miss Penny blew out a breath and crossed her arms over her chest.

Dad shot her a warning look. "I couldn't be sorrier for my actions and am standing before each of you asking forgiveness."

Miss Penny's hand came up to her mouth like she had to cover it to stop from blurting something out.

"It's the way I see it," Dad said.

Miss Penny threw her hands up in the air. "Talk about the separation, for heaven's sake. Or I will."

Dad stood there for a long moment. He shook his head. "Through no fault of her own, your mother wasn't sure she made the right decision in marrying me. She asked for time off from the marriage to figure things out. She wanted a break and I told her to take all the time she needed. She was gone three months when I met Kurt's mother, who I cared about very much."

Brielle squeezed Dalton's hand for support.

"Long story short, your mother said she made a terrible mistake and asked if she could come home. I believed in my heart the marriage was over when I didn't hear from her, but I loved her. My wife wanted to come home. And even though I'd started moving on, I knew in my heart that what we had was special." He studied Kurt. "Which doesn't lessen what I felt for your mother. Our relationship still had the shine on it, and it was special in its own way. When I told your mother that my wife wanted to come home, she understandably got upset. To the point she asked me never to call her again. I didn't. It was my brother Donny who told me about you after your mother gave birth. She wouldn't have anything to do with me when I tried to arrange a meeting. I'd hurt her too much. She sent a message that said if I cared about her at all, I would walk away and never look back. Then, she cut me to the quick when she said her son wasn't mine."

Kurt seemed to be taking it all in. His gaze was steady on his daughter, Paisley.

"I pushed it out of my mind best as I could. But, it ate

away at me from the inside out. I wanted to respect her wishes but I also wanted to contribute financially to my child and get to know you. I wanted a relationship. I've made many mistakes in my life but none I regret so much as turning a blind eye toward you and your mother. I imagine her pride stopped her from ever reaching out to me. And I hate that both of you suffered because I didn't know how to step up in the right way. It's my hope, Kurt, that you can truly forgive me. I don't deserve it, but I'd like to be there for you and my granddaughter from here on out."

Kurt ducked his head, chin to chest. He sniffed, then coughed to cover.

"Paisley needs all the family she can get." He kept his head low when he said, "And I do too. If everyone can accept us, we'd be honored to be part of the family."

The sounds of chairs scraping against the tile as everyone stood up and started making their way toward Kurt and his daughter echoed. Dalton thought about how much his father tried to protect his wife. She was gone and, somehow, had reached saint-like status with her husband. No wonder his father never remarried. It must be impossible to compete with a ghost.

BRIELLE WAS STRUCK by Mr. McGannon's speech. His love for his family came shining through. He also protected his wife without question. Her mind snapped to Dalton. He'd lost the person he planned to spend the rest of his life with *and* their child.

There was no way she could compete with that. As much as she believed Dalton deserved to be happy, he may never be able to allow it. She'd seen the torment in his father's eyes, the evidence that he'd never gotten over losing his wife even after all these years. That kind of devotion might be rare in the general world, but it was abundant here on the ranch.

She let go of Dalton's hand. She'd be kidding herself if she thought he'd be any different.

One of his brothers walked over to him. She was pretty certain it was Ryan. Definitely one of the older boys, now men.

Bandit wandered down the hallway and she followed while Dalton was distracted with his family. The doorbell rang and Dalton came jogging toward her.

His face pinched, eyebrows drawn together as he studied her face. "Everything okay?" He stopped beside her.

She mustered a smile. "Fine. Just reliving last night a little bit." It wasn't untrue. It also wasn't the whole story.

The doorbell dinged again.

"Hold on." He didn't seem convinced by her quick explanation. He held up a finger as he jogged backward toward the door. She'd never quite mastered the backward jog, but then she didn't have the athletic ability of a McGannon, either.

He turned right at the door as she heard the sound of a TV in the den. She'd been in this house dozens of times years ago, so she didn't figure anyone would mind if she followed the sound.

The TV boomed in the den and a familiar name caught her attention, Sophie Freedland. The lawyer from work was being discussed.

"A tragic accident or murder?" The brightly dressed and extremely polished news anchor clasped her hands together and leaned into her desk. "Once believed to be an accident, it is now believed the death of Sophie Freedland involves foul play."

Didn't that make the hairs on Brielle's arms prickle.

Dalton and the sheriff must have followed the sound, too, because they stood to either side of her.

"It turns out, the lawyer was having an affair. According to her husband Adrian, his wife was trying to break off the relationship so the two of them could work on their marriage."

A picture of Adrian Freedland popped up on the screen. He had a familiar face.

"That's him."

"Who?"

"That's the man I saw. The other night when I went up to the office. He was there," Brielle said.

"Which night was that?" The sheriff perked up.

Brielle leaned her head back and closed her eyes. Let's see, it was Friday by now. And she'd been home for two days after her visit to work. "Tuesday. The security system was already down and we were told not to come back the next day. They said we should work from home. Then, the notice of the accident came out. I'd assumed there might be other problems with the building."

"That's the night Sophie Freedland died," the sheriff said. What she didn't say was that put him on the scene of the crime the night of Sophie's accident. "Excuse me for a second."

The sheriff disappeared down the hallway.

"Do you think the guy she was having an affair with killed her? He would know about the security cameras not working," she asked Dalton.

"You can put her husband on the scene the night she

died. If she was having an affair, her husband might have been mad when he went up to her work."

The sheriff returned. "Are you one hundred percent certain the man on the television was in the building that night?"

"Positive. Runner's build. Sandy-brown hair. We literally walked right past each other. He held the door for me."

"Did he show any signs of nervousness?"

"No, well, wait a minute. He was sweaty. I thought he ran down the stairs. I didn't think anything of it with the elevator's condition." Brielle gasped when realization dawned. She could have bumped into a murderer moments after he'd killed his wife.

"Why? Didn't police speak to him after his wife's death?" she asked, still trying to process.

"Yes. He lied. Said he was home all night with their two-year-old daughter and never left the house."

"It was nighttime. She would have been asleep. But would he leave her alone?" Brielle couldn't even begin to unpack the fact a father could leave his child alone in a house and then murder the child's mother.

"To commit murder?" The sheriff nodded. "I'm afraid I've seen just about everything in my line of work." She had the stress lines to prove it. "Can you come down to my office and give a statement that you saw him at your office building on the evening of the murder?"

"Of course." A cold chill raced down her back. She'd told the man to have a good night after he'd killed his wife.

Her brain couldn't begin to fathom it.

"The local sheriff is sending a deputy to Mr. Freedland's residence. I have to head back to the office for a meeting," the sheriff began.

"What about Dad?" Dalton asked.

"I'll have to come back. This is urgent." She excused herself and mumbled something into her radio as she headed down the hallway toward the kitchen.

"Can we go now and get it over with?" Brielle was ready to put that part behind her. The writing on the wall was that Adrian Freedland had remembered her, too. So many pieces clicked together. The fact that he was a coward. Any man who could push his wife down an elevator shaft fit into that category. Worse yet, she was the mother of his child.

Brielle couldn't begin to fathom what this would do to that little girl's future. She gasped. "You don't think he would hurt their daughter, do you?"

16

D alton beat the sheriff to her office. He and Brielle were seated in a conference room where they were offered something to drink while they waited.

He'd felt a wall come up in between him and Brielle in the kitchen at the big house and was still trying to figure out what had happened. The silence between them was worse than a knife to his chest.

This wasn't the time or place to ask why. Logically, he should be able to let it go. But he couldn't. She stirred feelings in him that he hadn't felt since...ever. She needed to know she was important to him. He had no idea what that meant exactly. But he wanted to figure it out.

He reached his hand over to hers, unsure of the response he'd get.

When skin touched skin, she relaxed into his touch.

Before he could open his mouth to speak, a radio buzzed in the hallway, and then the sheriff walked in.

"Sorry to keep you waiting."

Brielle brought the sheriff up to date on what happened last night. Then, she gave her statement about seeing Adrian Freedland on the night of the murder. The sheriff wrote out the statement and then looked up at them.

"Sophie Freedland's parents showed up at Austin PD this morning, claiming their daughter had confided in them she had plans to leave her husband. There was an affair on her part, but it was over a long time ago. Mr. Freedland had threatened his wife that if she left and took their daughter, he'd hunt her down and kill them both. They feared for their daughter's life, but she reassured them he was just blowing off steam and didn't mean it. When police visited his home, they were suspicious, but a neighbor testified to seeing his vehicle parked at the house all night. It never moved. Apparently, he'd been keeping records of his mileage for work and his mileage matched up with his log."

"He has access to a black or navy-blue SUV," Dalton stated. "I've only seen it early in the morning before first light and at night, so I can't be certain on the color. The front bumper rammed into a red sports car owned by Kevin Roland, so there would be damage there. I believe Adrian Freedland was behind the wheel."

"Can you give a description of the driver?"

"No," he admitted. "I'm guessing he's at large."

"That's correct."

"And the little girl?" Brielle asked.

"She is believed to be with him."

Brielle gasped.

Dalton squeezed her hand for support. He shifted his gaze to Brielle. "It might be best if you stay at the ranch for a few days. Give law enforcement a chance to track this guy down."

"I have bad news in that department. A search of his

premises revealed his passport is missing. He has ties across the border." Sheriff Justice looked from Dalton to Brielle. "You should definitely keep your guard up, though. We have no idea what he's capable of."

Commotion in the hallway caught the sheriff's attention. She excused herself.

Sounds of a woman crying echoed down the hallway.

"Please, find my grandbaby, Sheriff." Those were the only words that needed to be spoken to know Sophie Freedland's parents were in the building.

"Can we stop by my house on the way to the ranch? If I'm staying for a couple of days, I'd like to bring my laptop and pick up a few supplies."

"Of course."

"Okay. Think we can go?"

"I don't see why not," he said.

They exited, letting the front desk know they were leaving. Dalton scanned the parking lot, looking for any glints of metal or signs something might be targeting them while they were exposed. He'd be looking over his shoulder until Adrian Freedland was behind bars.

The drive to Brielle's house was uneventful. There were no vehicles out front or suspicious activity around the house.

Brielle led the way inside. It was the middle of the day, so the place had plenty of sunshine streaming through the windows. Dalton basically became Brielle's shadow, hanging out in whichever room she was in.

"I need to pitstop in the restroom before the drive back to the ranch," he said.

Her face muscles had relaxed and some of the tension of the day seemed to be easing up.

"I'll run upstairs and grab my toiletries. Meet you back

in the living room," she said. She'd been walking fine, and her hip seemed to have improved.

"Sound good. I'll only be a second." He moved to the hallway bathroom as she ran upstairs.

He'd barely unzipped his pants when he heard footsteps pounding out a frantic rhythm on the way downstairs.

And then Brielle screamed.

Dalton raced into the other room as a sandy-brown figure enclosed his arms around her. She threw her head back, headbutting the intruder, and then twisted her body. He grunted but didn't lose his grip on her arm.

She tumbled to the floor and he dove on top of her.

Another scream ripped through his chest. A child's voice. Dalton's heart literally sank to his toes.

Dalton dove on the man's back, dug his arms around Adrian's body, forcing space in between Adrian and Brielle so she could scoot out of the way. She was bottom of the pile, so Dalton spun around onto his back, taking Adrian with him.

"The girl," he shouted to Brielle. The cries were steady, loud, and heartbreaking.

"Get off me or we'll all die," Adrian ground out.

"What's that supposed to mean?" Dalton didn't figure Adrian was in a position to give orders.

"He strapped a bomb to her chest and blocked her from leaving my bedroom." There was so much anguish in Brielle's voice. "I didn't want to leave her, but I couldn't get her out. What should I do?"

Dalton had at least a half foot of height on this guy, maybe more. But at least fifty pounds of muscle. He tossed him onto his front, rolled on top of him, pinning the guy with his knees.

"What did you see?" he asked Brielle who was already on the phone with the sheriff's office.

She gave a quick rundown and then set the phone aside. "Dispatch wants to keep the line open until the sheriff gets here. If anything changes, she wants us to shout it out."

"We need to check on the baby."

"I'll go." Brielle started toward the stairs.

"Hold on." He delivered a knockout punch honed by years of roughhousing with his brothers and cousins. "Do you have rope or anything I can use to tie him up?"

"Um, yes. Kitchen drawer." She disappeared and then returned with a roll of duct tape.

It didn't take long to bind the man's hands and feet. He'd wake up in a minute and Dalton didn't need him going anywhere except jail after the sheriff arrived.

"He's desperate and he's a coward," Dalton said to Brielle.

"You don't think the bomb is real."

He shook his head and then started toward the stairs. She followed. He stopped her with a hand up. "It's just a guess. I'm not a hundred percent."

"I think you're right. He would have killed her by now if he didn't want her around. And the grandparents said he threatened to Sophie because she was going to take his child away."

Dalton nodded. "I'd still feel better if you stayed down here."

"He's not going anywhere and I'm not letting you go up there by yourself."

Dalton issued a sharp sigh before giving a quick nod. He reached for her hand at the same time she reached for his. They linked their fingers and took the stairs at a good clip.

The baby was at the door, crying so hard that her face had turned red. She was trying to shove her hand in her mouth, he assumed to soothe herself. Some type of device was strapped onto her chest.

Taking in a deep breath, Dalton moved toward the kid. She reached her little hands toward Brielle and his heart melted right then and there. Other than being terrified, the little girl was clean and had on a matching outfit. Care had been taken to brush her hair. As much as Adrian Freedland was a jerk, he wouldn't harm this kid.

Brielle picked up the child and Dalton pulled the device off of her. It was makeshift, crude. An old clockface strapped against a metal backing. And all for show.

Sirens sounded out front. A couple of vehicles pulled up as Dalton, Brielle, and the baby navigated the stairs. The little girl's round cheeks were streaked with tears.

Adrian Freedland shook his head, like he was trying to shake off a fog. In the next seconds, the sheriff breached the doorway, weapon pointed and on the ready.

"He's taped up," Dalton immediately said.

She holstered her weapon and moved toward the perp.

"The bomb was a hoax. It's okay," he said.

Brielle tried to soothe the baby by softly singing. The little girl was down to a low cry and occasional hiccup.

"Her grandparents followed me. They're waiting outside," Sheriff Justice said.

"They've been waiting long enough for this angel's safe return," Brielle said. It was Dalton's turn to follow her. And he did.

The baby's disposition changed when she saw her grandparents. Her body started rocking and they embraced the little angel.

"Thank you," the grandfather said as his wife took the child from Brielle's arms.

"I'm just glad she's safe," Dalton said. A few hot tears rolled down his own cheeks.

∼

SENSING this was one of those grab-the-bull-by-the-horns moments, Brielle turned to Dalton. Losing him wasn't an option and he needed to know how she felt. He needed to know all the facts so he could make the best decision. She hoped that meant talking about their next step.

Dating?

Well, now she really was going crazy. They'd gone from zero to a hundred miles an hour in a matter of days. But she did know him. She'd known him for the better part of her life and she knew how deeply she cared about him. This wasn't a fly by night fling. This felt like the real deal, which was strange because it was unlike anything she'd ever felt before. And what was happening between them was too big to be ignored.

He could reject her. He could walk away. He could never look back. She might suffer the humiliation of being turned down and turned away. But at least she would know. She would walk away with her head held high with the knowledge she'd left her heart on the table. And maybe she couldn't compete with a ghost, but she'd never know if she didn't give him the option to fight for them.

Tears streaked her eyes, but she was done with those. There'd been enough sadness recently for a thousand lifetimes. This was about staring down that bull—that fear of rejection—and not backing away for a second.

Show no fear was her new motto. And that lasted about a minute.

"Dalton. I need to tell you something."

He stopped but didn't turn around.

Pulling on all her courage, she started, "We've known each other a long time."

His shoulder muscles tensed, and she had to fight to keep herself from reaching out, from touching his back, from memorizing every muscle. Nothing in his body language said he welcomed this conversation.

And yet he didn't walk away, either.

"I've never felt like this about anyone else, Dalton..." She took in a fortifying breath. "And I think you feel the same way."

She was going out on a limb, but he didn't argue or tell her she was wrong.

So, she continued.

"Since what we have going on between us is special, I think we should give it a chance and see where it takes us." She already had a destination in mind but forever started with one step forward. "So, what I need to know is...what do you think?"

Dalton issued a sharp sigh. He whirled around on her with the force of a hurricane. She expected him to say something even if it was to object to everything she'd just said or set her straight. Tell her that he didn't feel the same way and that she was kidding herself.

Being bold wasn't usually her forte. But this was her life. This was the man she loved...loved?

Yes, loved.

And he needed to know that too.

"I'm in love with you, Dalton."

"Don't be." His words were like knives to her chest except that they were hollow. There was no emotion behind them.

"It wasn't a choice for me. I'm sorry if it is for you."

He stood there, hands fisted at his sides, looking like he was about to charge a bull.

"I'll only hurt you."

"Why?"

"Because I can only go so far. It won't be enough."

"What if it already is?"

A look passed behind his eyes that she couldn't quite pinpoint.

So, she decided to capitalize on it.

"I love you, Dalton. That's not going to change. We can go our separate ways but that doesn't mean I'll forget you. I'll understand that you're making another choice and I'll work to get over you. But nothing in me wants to."

"You'd be better off."

"I don't agree."

He brought his hand up to rake his fingers through his hair. "Why are you so stubborn?"

That made her crack a smile. It didn't translate and she decided not to answer.

"Why do you want to be with me?"

"I already told you."

"It makes no sense. I'll hurt you."

"I'm not perfect either, Dalton. Stick around and you'll figure that out real fast."

"You? You're exactly perfect. You're the definition of perfect. I've never met anyone more perfect than you."

"Then, why not take a chance on us?"

If he sighed any harder, he might explode.

"Is that what you really want?" There was a hint of vulnerability behind that steel façade.

"Yes. Is that so bad or so wrong?"

Dalton didn't answer and for a split second she wondered if he was debating walking away. And then he came charging toward her. She did the only thing she could think of...held her ground.

He stopped not two inches in front of her face before bringing his hands up to cup her cheeks and bringing his lips down on hers in a kiss that made her feel like she'd just been claimed on the most primal level. Goosebumps ran up and down her arms and her stomach freefell like she'd just jumped off a cliff.

She brought her hands up to his chest, digging her fingers into solid muscle, searching for purchase, for something to ground her to the spot. Electricity hummed through her body.

And when he pulled back, he had the most intense look in his eyes.

"You should know that I intend to play for keeps."

Her heart sang.

"So do I."

"Good. Because I love you, Brielle. I'm head over heels in love with you. I've never been more out of my league or comfort zone. And it's never felt more like exactly the place I should be right now. You are the person I want to do life with—the rest of my life. You are the person I want to wake up to every morning and can't wait to come home to at night. But, I'm a work in progress. I'm still learning to let go of the past and let you in." Her heart freefell when he looked at her. There was so much vulnerability there. "I'm lost without you. I love you and I'd be honored if you would agree to marry me."

"I don't expect perfection and I'm far from it no matter what you just said. We're going to make mistakes and that's perfectly okay. As long as we follow our hearts and stay true to the way we feel, we'll be able to work everything else out." She locked onto those beautiful eyes of his. "And, yes, Dalton. My answer is yes. I would love to be your wife."

17

EPILOGUE

R eed McGannon started toward the kitchen in the big house where he overheard two of his cousins talking.

"Do you think there's any chance he's responsible?" Declan asked Levi.

"No idea."

"How messed up would that be?" Declan continued. He was talking about Reed's father and his possible involvement in the accident that led to their father's coma.

Levi was quiet.

"What about Reed and the others? Have you talked to any of them yet?" Declan asked.

"No. No one is bringing it up and I don't know what to say now that Uncle Donny has been arrested." Levi's voice was hushed. The fact shouldn't bother Reed as much as it did. Because how long before the family that had been so close-knit growing up fractured?

It was Reed's father, after all, that had been arrested. It was his father that was in jail. And Reed hadn't been able to force himself to visit.

Why?

Wasn't that an easy enough task? Go to the jail and ask his father if he had anything to do with the accident that had almost cost the man who'd raised him his life?

"Has anyone been out to see Uncle Donny since his arrest?" Declan asked.

"Not that I know of. But, you know, it's a sore subject. One that I'm not planning to bring up with the others," Levi said. He lowered his voice and said something that Reed couldn't quite pick up on.

Standing there, listening, brought a wave of guilt. In a perfect world, he wouldn't have to spy on his cousins to find out what was on their minds. It didn't exactly feel good. Nothing about the situation involving his father and theirs was warm and fuzzy.

Reed wanted to be able to charge into the next room and stand up for his father, take his side. Reality? It was difficult to defend a man who'd walked away from his kids, gambled away a fortune, and then came back when he had nothing left.

A question nagged Reed. Had he inherited his father's weaknesses? No one could deny genetics played a big role in a person's makeup. Whether it was nature or nurture, Reed wasn't qualified to say. Statistics proved, time and time again, people followed in the footsteps laid before them by their family members.

It was easy for Levi and Declan. Their father was the good McGannon. What happened to the other branch of the family tree?

"I'm not planning to say anything to our cousins," Levi's voice raised to an audible level.

The sound of the back door opening and then closing, then feet shuffling into the room caused him to freeze.

"Oh, hello. What are you boys talking about all huddled up over the sink?" Miss Penny's voice was rain in a draught. She was the constant in the family. Surrogate mother to both sides of the family tree. A bright spot of commonality between cousins.

"We were just talking about how incredible your supper was last night," Levi said quickly.

There was a beat of silence. Reed could imagine the expression on Miss Penny's face. Eyes narrowed. Lips clamped. Her fisted hands were probably planted on her hips.

"Next thing you know, you'll be trying to sell me a bridge," she finally quipped. "Fess up."

A sharp sigh came from one of his cousins.

"We were just talking about Uncle Donny's situation and the rift it's been causing in the family," Levi said.

Miss Penny sucked in a burst of air. "I hate what this situation is doing to my boys."

"I just wish he'd never come back to town," Declan said.

"Don't say that," Miss Penny admonished. "Whatever else he is, the man is still father to your cousins."

"Is he, though?" Declan's attitude didn't sit well no matter how true the question was.

Again, the urge to stand up for Reed's old man surged and then withered inside him. He wanted to be able to come to his father's defense. What could he say? His father wasn't worthless? There was no way he would have tried to kill his only brother?

It wasn't that long ago the man came to Reed and asked a question that had been stuck in his thoughts ever since on replay.

"What do you think about going to a lawyer to fight for more of the ranch?" His father had asked.

Reed's face had twisted up in a mix of confusion and disgust. "What right do you have to ask that question?"

"Birthright. I have just as much right to this business as my brother."

Reed had wanted to follow up with the question, "Do you?" But he'd kept his mouth shut.

When he told his father that he didn't think they'd win, what he should have said was they had no right to try. Uncle Clive had built the business into the million-dollar operation it was today.

"Have you worked the land just as much as your cousins?" His father had asked.

"That's not the point." In Reed's mind, his father was so far off base; he wasn't even in the parking lot.

"Educate me on what is then?" His father's mood soured. The conversation wasn't going the way he wanted and his expression made that clear. Face pinched, he'd continued, "You and your brothers have worked yourselves to the bone building a business my brother plans to leave to his kids. Do you really think he's going to give you and your brothers the keys to the kingdom? Do you really believe that? Because I haven't heard him say it once. Not one time that has he hinted to me that he plans to take care of you boys in the way you deserve."

Reed had folded his arms across his chest.

"What's in it for you?" he'd asked.

His father recoiled like he'd been slapped.

"What are you asking, son?"

"Say my brothers and I end up with a bigger piece of the pie." He had no intention of telling his father about the document he'd been shown giving them equal shares of McGannon Herd. "What is it to you?"

"I've been doing a little research on my own. If we decided to... And I'm not saying we will, mind you, but if we did decide to challenge my brother in court, we could take what's ours."

The sad thought that came to mind was that his father wanted more gambling money. Uncle Clive had given his brother a job but it came with a salary, not a piece of the company. He'd reassured Reed and his brothers their inheritance was safe.

"Count me out. The others too. We don't want any part of your schemes." Had those words pushed his father over the edge? Caused him to take another tact? A deadly one?

There was an odd thing about an inheritance. Someone had to die. It was a morbid thought at best. Reed loved his uncle. The man had raised him, protected him, and was still looking out for him. He wanted nothing but good things for Uncle Clive.

Reed's guilt came with the fact he was responsible for his father's arrest. He'd gone to the sheriff and given a statement. He'd been the one to implicate his father. He'd volunteered the information. And the guilt was a crushing weight on his chest.

TO CONTINUE READING Reed and Addison's story, click here.

ALSO BY BARB HAN

Kidnapped at Christmas

Murder and Mistletoe

Bulletproof Christmas

For more of Barb's books, visit www.BarbHan.com.

ABOUT THE AUTHOR

Barb Han is a USA TODAY and Publisher's Weekly Best-selling Author. Reviewers have called her books "heartfelt" and "exciting."

Barb lives in Texas—her true north—with her adventurous family, a poodle mix and a spunky rescue who is often referred to as a hot mess. She is the proud owner of too many books (if there is such a thing). When not writing, she can be found exploring Manhattan, on a mountain either hiking or skiing depending on the season, or swimming in her own backyard.

Sign up for Barb's newsletter at www.BarbHan.com.

Made in United States
Troutdale, OR
08/03/2023

11798682R00105